P9-DWD-538

AND
AFTER
MANY
DAYS

AND
AFTER
MANY
DAYS

A Novel

JOWHOR ILE

TIM
DUGGAN
BOOKS

NEW YORK

Published in the United States by Tim Duggan Books, an imprint of the Crown Publishing Group, a division of Penguin Random House LLC, New York.
www.crownpublishing.com

TIM DUGGAN BOOKS and the Crown colophon are trademarks of Penguin Random House LLC.

Library of Congress Cataloging-in-Publication Data is available upon request.

ISBN 978-1-101-90314-8
eBook ISBN 978-1-101-90315-5

Printed in the United States of America

Book design by Lauren Dong
Jacket design by Michael Morris

10 9 8 7 6 5 4 3 2 1

First Edition

For my mother and my father, Nma *ya* Pagem
Mercy Ebere and Edwin James Ile,
stars in my firmament.

CHAPTER ONE

Paul turned away from the window and said he needed to go out at once to the next compound to see his friend. It was a Monday afternoon in the rainy season of 1995. Outside, the morning shower had stopped and the sun was gathering strength, but water still clung to the grass on the lawn. "I'm going to Fola's house," he said again to his brother, Ajie, who was lying on the couch, eyes closed, legs hooked up the back of the chair. If Ajie heard, he gave no sign.

Ajie sighed as a woman presenter's voice came on the radio, cutting through the choral music. "Why do they always interrupt at the best part?"

Paul floundered by the door as though he had changed his mind; then he bent to buckle his sandals, slung on his backpack, left the house, and did not return.

At least that is one way to begin to tell this story.

Things happen in clusters. They would remember it as the year the Mile Three ultramodern market burned down in the middle of the night. The year the trade fair came to town and the Port Harcourt city council, in preparation for the major event, commissioned long brightly painted buses that ran for cheap all the way from Obigbo to Borokiri (a full hour's journey for a mere two naira!). It was the year of the poor. Of rumors, radio announcements, student riots, and sudden disappearances. It was also the year news reached them of their home village, Ogibah, that five young men had been shot dead by the square in broad daylight. The sequence of events that led to this remained open to argument.

Ajie stretched out and yawned, then dropped his arm and let it dangle from where he lay on the couch. He heard the gate creak as Paul let himself out, and the house fell back to the radio music and the sound of Bibi, their middle sister, blow-drying her hair in the bathroom.

Ajie and Bibi were due back in school that weekend. Their tin trunks were packed, school day uniforms already ironed and hanging, waiting in wardrobes. Ma went through the school lists, as she always did before the start of each term, checking to see that everything had been bought. Paul had finished his final school certificate exams in June, so he stayed at home while Ajie and Bibi spent hot afternoons at Mile One Market with Ma, buying school supplies for the term: textbooks, notebooks, buckets, mosquito nets, provisions, T-squares, drawing boards, four figure tables, cutlasses, brooms, and jerricans.

Their father, Bendic, had decided that since Bibi's school was on the outskirts of town, she would be dropped off on Saturday evening. Ajie's school was four hours away, so they had reserved all of Sunday for his journey. The blue Peugeot 504 station wagon was sent to the mechanic for servicing. For a whole afternoon their driver, Marcus, sat under the guava tree and read a paper and fanned himself, and when the cloud changed face, he carried his seat into the gatehouse, where Ismaila had a little pot set on the stove. The pot boiled and the lid clattered against the rim, letting go a fold of steam that escaped through the windows into the trees outside, and the sharp scent of *dadawa* sauce reached toward the main house.

☒

The day before, Bendic had called Ajie and Bibi into his study as he prepared letters to their guardians. Bibi's guardian was an agile, muscular woman whom Ajie had seen once during a visit to Bibi's school; he had assumed from the woman's air of personal authority and wide, relentless hips that she was the school's matron. Bibi later told him she was a mere agriculture teacher and nothing more. Ajie's guardian, Mr. Onabanjo— school bursar, head of accounts—was far too busy, thankfully, to nose about, as some guardians did their wards. Bendic's pen scratched noisily across the smooth lineless paper—curved generous loops, downward slants, and furious dots at the end of sentences. For a moment, Ajie imagined himself one of his father's clients as he stood by the large teak table, taking in the heavy green of the damask curtain, the black buff leather chair, the scattering of papers held down by paper holders, and imposingly behind Bendic, the hard shelves with rows of thick volumes. Their father often brought his work home, but he rarely discussed the cases. Ajie imagined how Bendic would speak to his clients: courteously, with a measured tone and lawyerly understanding.

Bendic's pen finally stopped moving. He handed them the letters and leaned back in his chair as they proofread. He often told them it was foolish and dangerous to carry a letter without knowing its content. "You might be carrying a document instructing that you be sold, and you wouldn't know it. *Won't read* and *can't read* land you at the same place." Bibi always laughed about this when their father wasn't there. She would yelp like someone from the TV. "How ridiculous!" she would say, shaking her head. "Who buys people, anyway? Who hands someone a letter saying that the mail carrier should be sold?"

By the evening of the day Paul disappeared, there was some concern regarding where he might be, but everyone believed he was on his way back, that he would show up at any minute. The creak from the gate each time was him. Bendic didn't go into his study to work for an hour or so, as he often did. He came out to the parlor and stood by the room dividers, buttoning his shirt, though his eyes were fixed on Ma. "I'm just going to walk to the gate," he said, and Ma nodded, murmuring a response but never looking away from the pile of papers she was marking on the dining table. She shuffled some and then set them aside. "Bibi, please see that the phone receiver is properly placed." Bibi picked up the receiver and dropped it gently. A click escaped, and then she picked it up again and replaced it, just to make sure.

Bendic came back a few minutes after. Ma looked up at the door hopefully as he walked in. "Nothing," Bendic said, "but there's still time."

They sat in the parlor until long after midnight. Twice the lights went out, but no one moved or even muttered "NEPA!" with the usual irritation. The lantern stationed in the passage stayed trimmed low, casting a yellow light beside the eddying shadow of the curtain hem. Generator engines started up in nearby compounds, one after another, and then together became a steady roar for several minutes until power was restored and ordinary quiet returned as the engines were killed off. The silence was so sudden and pure, it seemed as if the clock on the parlor wall had come to life, the slender second hand scratching its halting way around like a cripple.

Bendic looked up at the clock. "It's way past your bedtime," he said to Bibi and Ajie. He took off his glasses and wiped the lenses slowly with the edge of his wrapper. "Wherever your brother is, he has probably decided to sleep there tonight. It's too late for him to be on the road. We will see him in the morning." Bendic said the last sentence with conviction, as if he had kept Paul somewhere safe for the night and would make sure to call him out in the morning.

Ajie found it easy to fold himself into Bendic's confidence: The calmness in his father's voice, the certainty, felt much better than the roar of noises in his own head. Bibi was standing behind the sofa where Ma sat, her hand on the headrest beside Ma's dark, straightened hair, and Ajie could tell Bibi didn't want to go to bed, either.

"But sleep where?" Ma's voice rose sharply. "Where could he have gone that he cannot return home tonight? I don't understand the meaning of this nonsense."

Bendic put his glasses back on. Ma looked at her wristwatch and then up at the clock on the parlor wall. "Paul knows how dangerous the roads can be at night, he knows," she muttered.

Ajie and Bibi shuffled off to their rooms, leaving their parents in the parlor. Ajie climbed into bed but was unable to sleep. He saw for the first time how high the bedroom ceiling was, and how long the curtains were, nearly grazing the floor beside Paul's bed. *In the morning, Paul will be home,* he thought as his eyes scanned the half-lit space between his bed and Paul's. The fluorescent light was on in the parlor; he didn't hear his parents speaking but for a long time kept his eyes on the white light that fell through the gap underneath his door, straining his ears, willing his parents to say something he could hear, or at least get up, turn off the light, and go to their room.

When he woke up in the morning, Ajie looked around the room, his gaze sweeping the corners. He got up and checked the foot of Paul's bed to see if his sandals or backpack had returned to their usual place, but there was nothing. Bendic was getting ready to go to the police station when Ajie came out of his room. He heard Bendic's voice and walked into his parents' bedroom, where Bendic was combing his hair before a standing mirror. His long-sleeved white shirt was tucked into his white underpants, sticking out above his hefty thighs. His black pinstriped suit was laid out on the bed.

"*Mbani-o*," Ajie greeted him. "Good morning."

Bendic held the comb away from his head as he responded. "How was your sleep?" he asked, and waited for Ajie to speak before he added, "I'm going to make a report at the police station." He picked up his trousers from the bed. "Mere formality." He put his legs into the trousers quickly and then reached for his shoes. "Maybe Paul will be home before I even get to the station." He told Ajie that Ma had driven to work to drop off keys and that she would return home as soon as she could.

"Once Paul returns," Bendic instructed Ajie, peering at his son's reflection in the mirror, "ring my office immediately—tell Bibi this, too—and if I'm not there, leave a message with my secretary. You hear me?"

Ma came in from work just before lunchtime. She stopped by the gate as she drove in and wound down the car window to speak to Ismaila. Ajie and Bibi stood from where they sat on the veranda steps and walked toward the driveway. Ajie knew she was asking Ismaila if Paul had returned. When she got into the house, she dropped her bag beside her on the sofa and slipped off her shoes. "Your brother has not returned," she said. Ajie shook his head. Bibi said no. Ma gave a light shrug and turned her lips downward the way people do when they don't know what to make of something.

They sensed something had gone wrong, but it was new, whatever it was, so no one knew how to hold it properly. *Not Paul,* everyone thought. It was not like Paul to get into trouble or give anyone reason to worry. He was the least scolded of the children, the most commended by teachers. Even Bibi, with her excellent grades, had been scolded once or twice by her teachers. One teacher explained to Bendic that although Bibi was a sensible girl, her occasional impulse to fall in with the wrong crowd had to be watched for and curtailed. Ajie made up for his siblings' good behavior: frequently fighting, reading novels during lessons, perpetually making noise. Teachers' remarks in his report card ranged from subtle complaints to terse rebukes: "A little careless in his work," "If he talks less, he will do better," "Lack of respect for school property and property of others," "Rude."

Paul, on the other hand, was always the exemplary firstborn; the letters from school to his parents were usually consent to let him travel to another state as part of the school debate team or for some intercollegiate sporting event. In JS3 he was appointed the school bell ringer, a position generally viewed as grooming for a future head-boy position.

Bendic stopped by the police station again on his way from work. Ma followed him into his room when he got home; Ajie couldn't hear more than a murmur from what he was saying to Ma. Ajie and Bibi hovered about the corridor, but in no time, the door handle rattled and Bendic came out of the bedroom. He went over to the dining table, where his food was laid out, and washed his hands. He molded the *eba* in his palm, but instead of dipping it in the soup, he rested his hand on the table, then returned the *eba* to the plate.

"Bibi," he said, and Bibi got up from where she had just gone to sit on the arm of a chair, "take the food back. Cover it, I will eat later."

That night Ma began making calls to friends. She spoke with caution, wording her questions carefully: Had they seen Paul? Had they heard anything about him? Had he come around to their place? He hadn't come home in nearly two days. Some people kept her longer on the phone, and Ma would respond, "I don't know. About twelve-thirty. We have reported it, but we are looking everywhere."

They sent word to family friends. Like the pendulum on their parlor wall, they swung to either end, dread and hope, but generally stayed in balance: no hysterical outbursts, no screaming and pounding the walls for answers, no silent bitter tears that soaked the pillow when you lifted your head in the morning. There was just stillness. Something quiet crept about the house, made you feel a sudden chill, and sprayed your arms and neck with unexpected goose bumps.

It was Auntie Julie's coming that in some way shook them all awake.

CHAPTER TWO

I f you'd ever lived in Port Harcourt, you would know what a wet, tiring month September could be. June and July are heavy rain months. The rains stomp through the city, throwing punches, felling trees, striking down electric poles overnight across roads so that early-bird motorists get stranded, their headlights trapped in the predawn wetness, counting on the help of passersby to move a fallen tree off the road, to pry out tires stuck in loam. By early August everyone, even the TV stations, celebrates the onset of "August break": two dry weeks of sharp sunlight, more or less. Wedding planners gauge and take advantage. On Saturday mornings, Trans Amadi Road clogs up with traffic. A tangle of cars, buses, trucks, and taxi motorbikes storms out from Garrison Junction to Nwaja Bridge, all the way to Elekahia. Various wedding parties run late for the service, hurrying the other way across town toward their reception venue.

Ajie once saw a bride, her dress blindingly white in the sunlight, her pineapple hairstyle tightly gelled and held down with a tiara, alight from a black Benz with visible encouragement from her cohort. They had flagged down an *okada* for her while she snaked her way through the traffic with her maid of honor on her tail. She hoisted up her satin dress (the maid of honor holding on to the chapel train) and then heaved herself onto the pillion of the motorbike to make her own wedding ceremony in time. There was the early gleam of sweat on her neck and forehead, and the bouquet of flowers in the grip of her left hand was pink and yellow and plastic.

Evening air swells from blaring microphones as churches set up camps in open fields for crusades and miracle revivals. The crowds spill out on the field; parked cars litter the adjacent roads. The congregation amasses before a makeshift stage with a wooden lectern mounted at the center, banners tied up and billowing behind it and all around. Voices rise in praise and worship; clap-hand choruses with keyboard accompaniment suffuse the cool evening air.

The heavy rains return soon after, but only briefly. By September they mellow. The skies open and drop water all day—drizzle this time, but the streets get flooded, drainages overflow, *okada* men in rain capes hang about under the eaves of roadside shops, shielding their motorcycles from the water, ignoring prospective passengers. Auntie Julie came in the drizzling rain when she heard Paul had disappeared. She banged on the gate, and when Ismaila let her in, she walked right past, her slippers in her hand, her wrapper dripping water all over the floor of the veranda as she made her way into the house.

She wasn't the first person to visit after hearing about Paul. Mr. Pepple, an integrated science teacher from Ma's school, was the first. He was a quiet-looking man with veins running sideways on his face from forehead to temple. He lived somewhere near Ordinance, not too far from the house, and Ma occasionally gave him lifts to Garrison Junction after work. He placed his sandals neatly beside the doormat and Ma protested. "Ah-ah! Please come inside with your shoes, I beg you." Mr. Pepple still left his sandals by the door, came inside, and took a seat.

Worry knotted his brows and thickened the veins that ran

from his temples into his receding hair. He must have heard everything there was to be heard from Ma, but he found it necessary to ask, "Any news?"

"No," Ma said, "we are still waiting." The police required forty-eight hours before they could declare Paul a missing person.

"God forbid!" he spat out. He looked like the sort of man for whom all strong emotions came out looking like anger. Ajie couldn't tell if he was angry that Paul was missing or angry with Paul for going missing or whether he was angry at all. Whichever way, it was clear his sympathy was with Ma.

"He can't be *missing*," Mr. Pepple said with conviction, relaxing his shoulders. "That's not your portion, my sister."

"He told his brother he was going over to our neighbor's house just across the road," Ma explained, looking at Ajie. Ajie confirmed with a nod. He was the last person to see Paul, the last person Paul spoke to; they always returned to that moment and settled on it as if the mystery had to be unearthed from there. "But our neighbors traveled over a week ago . . ." She drifted off. "I don't understand it. What would he tell a lie for? Or maybe he was going somewhere else and said that in error?"

Mr. Pepple allowed some time to pass before he leaned over for the bottle of malt on the tray before him. He had said he didn't need a glass; he held the brown bottle by the neck and tilted his head back. The man's throat worked itself up and down as he swallowed another mouthful of the sweet, dark malt drink. Then he took a breather and rested the bottle on the tray. "Does he follow bad friends?" Mr. Pepple asked.

"No," Ma replied, "Paul is not like that."

Ajie was irritated by Mr. Pepple's silly questions, but he couldn't help noticing how tired the man looked in his fading blue shirt: a little disheveled, like an item picked up and dropped all of a sudden.

"How are the roads?" Ma asked. Over the last few days, there had been student demonstrations that had gradually escalated. Apart from the roadblocks set up by the students, police vans were burned, students shot at—shot dead—no one was sure exactly what had happened.

"No problem at all," Mr. Pepple answered. "I think the police have calmed things down a bit. Nothing happened in the house?" he asked. By which he meant had there been a quarrel that might have led to Paul disappearing. Ma said no again, her hands faceup on her lap. There were those stories of children who fell out with their parents or stole things from home and ran off with friends for a week or two. Like the prodigal son, they always returned, disgraced, in a bad state, and begging for mercy.

"Did Paul carry anything, a bag or something? Who saw him when he was leaving?" Mr. Pepple was asking all these questions when Bibi pushed a thick encyclopedia off the dining table, and it hit the floor with a loud thud that made everyone jump. Ma asked Bibi what that was, and Bibi gave some indistinct response. Ma continued, explaining to Mr. Pepple that Paul had gone with his school bag. She further explained that it wasn't unusual. Paul sometimes had cassettes, videotapes, magazines, books, or video games in his bag when he went over to see his friend.

"Just number eight here," Ma said, pointing in the general direction of their neighbor's. Ajie's eyes followed the stretch of her hand as she pointed to the parlor wall, and he imagined Paul trapped within it, hearing them worry aloud about him but unable to speak or free himself.

Disbelief hung across Mr. Pepple's face. Ajie would come to spot this reflex in people—their keen questions, then the sudden letting go, as if something in the story didn't add up but they were prepared to accept it all the same.

Auntie Julie wasn't like this. She fell into Ma's arms once she got into the parlor and cried out with a loud voice. Her hands gripped Ma around the waist. Ma stood stiff in Auntie Julie's grip, her own clothes taking up water.

"Come and change your clothes, Julie," Ma said, "before cold enters your body." When they came out, Auntie Julie was wearing one of Ma's *boubous*, made from green *adire*. The loose gown with wide-open arms seemed a little too big for her.

Julie sat on the sofa and shivered her legs while Ma went into the kitchen to make her a hot drink. She asked Bibi to get her a blanket from the bedroom, then she began talking aloud, to no one in particular, about how devastating it must be to carry a child in your womb for nine months and then this. These children have no sense. How could he just go somewhere without telling anyone? Where did he go? They just don't understand what a mother feels. Her soliloquy was about to flow into mournful singing when Ma came out of the kitchen with a steaming mug of Bournvita. She handed Auntie Julie the chocolate drink and warned her that it was hot.

Auntie Julie took the mug from Ma. "Thank you," she murmured, and immediately placed it on the side stool as if the drink were getting in the way of something much more important. "These children." Auntie Julie sighed, looking at Bibi and then Ajie as if they might have it in them to behave the same way Paul had. If their brother could act in this manner, God only knew what to expect from the pair of them. Ma, already

burdened with her own worry, had to play consoler, silent ar-
biter in the room, and protector of the two children; her voice
also took on a warm braveness to soothe Auntie Julie.

"It's okay," she said, "Paul will come home. We will find
him."

"Hmm." Auntie Julie nodded. "How many days now?"

Ma put her fingers up. "Nearly three days now. About
twelve-thirty Monday afternoon was when he left."

"Three days!" Auntie Julie's voice hit the ceiling. She shook
three fingers in front of Ma's face. "Jesus Christ! I thought it
was only last night. You know these quiet ones. They are the
ones who surprise you." Bibi left the parlor. Ajie just sat there
looking up at the clock. They were expecting Bendic from the
police station.

Later that night, after Bendic had returned from the station, they all sat in silence before the television. Auntie Julie was
sunk into the sofa, folded inside Ma's oversize green *boubou,*
the heavy embroideries snaking their way all around the neck.
She shook her legs rhythmically where she sat, then made a fist
and held up her jaw with it. Ma went into the kitchen, and Ajie
heard her lock the back door. She did not return to the parlor
immediately, and Ajie wondered what she was doing. All evening, her face had a calm, steely cast while she made dinner,
and called Bibi every now and then to pass her that spoon or
that ladle, or to "sit down and pound the pepper."

Ma was not the type of woman, Ajie thought, you could find
brooding with her hand under her chin or weeping silently into
the kitchen sink. She was their mother, a biology teacher, the
vice principal of a boys' school that once was the most notori-

ous in town. A school she had turned around single-handedly in a year. Twice, the parents' association had opposed and pressured the Ministry of Education to reverse her transfer. Twice, they had canvassed and rallied funds to keep the parent/teacher scheme she'd set up from going under.

Ma returned to the parlor, wiping her hand on a napkin, just as the final news recap came on at eleven. Government, the newsreader said, had gone into dialogue with the university students regarding their grievances. All citizens, the man continued, were being admonished to "give peace a chance, to refrain from violent, nefarious activities, and to engage in dialogue with government for the betterment of the state."

The national anthem was played by a full military band. On the TV screen was a fluttering flag hoisted high: bands of rich green on either end of the flag and a white band in the middle with the coat of arms printed on it. The pledge was recited by a choir of unseen children, and then the station went off the air.

There was silence and intermittent bursts of conversation. All Ajie could think of was Auntie Julie weeping that afternoon as though Paul were dead; Bibi sitting for so long in the dining area until it was dark and she became one with the woolly shadows of the shelves. And now there was Bendic with a newspaper adrift in his lap, although he had put his glasses away. Auntie Julie shifted in her seat. She let out a deep sigh and leaned back in the sofa. For a moment she seemed to have dropped into sleep, and then the song came out of her in a low stream, as if from some secret speakers hidden beneath her seat. Her eyes were now closed.

The steadfast love of the Lord never ceaseth
His mercies never come to an eeeeend . . .

Her voice glided over the high notes and her hands were held together in a tight ball, between her legs, on the slope of her gown. Bendic leaned back and watched. Bibi, Ma, Ajie, all sat as if uncertain of their position—should they join in or remain mere spectators? Were they being called on to take roles in this play they weren't familiar with? Ajie felt his bladder fill up, and he knew he would have to get up and go to the bathroom. Auntie Julie leaned to one side as she rummaged through the pocket of the *boubou,* the song still coming out of her, and brought out a white hankie that she spread out over her head. She looked at Bibi in a way that perhaps should have persuaded Bibi to find a covering for her head as a woman in the posture of prayer, but Bibi sat there, her lips barely moving. The song was common enough, even for irregular churchgoers. Ma joined in. Ajie stood up, looked at Bendic as if asking to be excused, then pointed toward the bathroom. Auntie Julie made a smooth segue into a church chorus:

> *He can never never change*
> *He can never never change*
> *He can never never change*
> *Jesus the same forever*
> *He can never never change*

In the bathroom, Ajie looked in the mirror and thought his face looked bigger than it really was. He heard Ma's voice rise as the singing continued. They sang the same chorus over and over, in different languages—Kalabari, Igbo, Yoruba, Ogoni. Ma's voice strained over the high notes, but she kept on, steady, pushing through by the sheer strength of her lungs. Her voice stood apart, raw and singular, like a howl in the forest. Ajie lifted the toilet lid and sat down. After the singing had died down, he stood up and flushed the toilet and then returned before the mirror to brush his teeth. He heard Auntie Julie say good night, and then the slow slap-slap of her rubber slippers as she walked past the bathroom door and down the corridor. He didn't hear Bibi leaving the parlor, but he heard the sharp click of her door when it closed.

Bendic was talking to Ma now. Ma interrupted, her voice tense, impatient. "No mortuary, please, Ben. You can check hospitals. Emergency units." He heard Ma snap her fingers. "God forbid—what are you thinking?" Bendic's low voice kept saying something back to her.

Ajie bared his teeth before the mirror the way people did in toothpaste commercials. He picked up Paul's toothbrush and ran his thumb over the bristles. Moist. He put it back in the cup. He then used his fingers to push the corners of his lips up as if to pull a smiley face. *If something really bad is happening,* Ajie thought, *is it possible to try to smile, even if it is only a pretend smile? And if you are able to smile when "something really bad" is happening, does that count? Could that be a sign that things will turn around for good?* He pushed the corners of his mouth upward. This time, three front teeth showed. He picked up Paul's brush again and ran his thumb over the bristles but wasn't sure anymore if the moisture was from the brush itself or just his own fingers.

Ajie awoke from a dream and looked across to Paul's bed, and there he was, carelessly asleep, covered in a blanket. He was lying on his chest with his face down, his hands folded over the pillow. Then he turned onto his side, drew up his legs, and held the blanket close around his neck; he stretched out his long legs across the bed and threw a sleepy arm over his face. Now he was on his front, with his legs drawn up under him like someone attempting to crouch. Then he lay still for a while. A person under a blanket could sometimes look like a camel, a camel with its hump, or a pitched tent under a dark desert sky. Paul stirred. Then the inky edges of the blanket became vague and wavy, as if he weren't there anymore. Outside, the moon moved and threw a light on the empty pillow. Ajie kept staring at the bed, willing Paul's form back on it, but he couldn't remember how Paul used to look while lying on his bed.

When Ajie got up in the morning, it was already bright, and he heard Ismaila's voice carry through from the front of the house, where he washed the car. The singing ended. Ajie didn't imagine that singing of any sort could occur when no one knew where Paul was.

Ma and Bendic didn't leave early for work, as they used to. On the windowsill beside Paul's bed (Paul had the window bed, since he was older), the blue beetle-shaped digital clock sat, its screen facing outside. What time was it? The forgotten dream came back to him. He was sitting with Auntie Julie by a well. She stood up to leave, then tripped over a bucket and fell into the well. He looked into the well and saw her head bobbing, water splashing around her. She wasn't shouting or crying for help. She just bobbed up, down, up, down, kicking and splashing the water with her hands. As if it were all planned, Ajie lifted the lid and covered the well and hooked it shut with a piece of metal. Muffled echoes of his name began to come from below, like someone shouting into a pillow. As he walked away from the scene, he looked up, and there was Paul sitting high in a nearby tree, looking down at him with accusation in his eyes.

It annoyed Ajie, now that he was awake, that it didn't occur to him to ask Paul where he had been those four days when everyone was looking for him.

Auntie Julie was getting ready to leave when Ajie walked into the parlor. She had changed into her own clothes and was holding a little bag in her hand. "You have woken up. Your sister is at the back of the house," Auntie Julie said somberly, as if Bibi were just the right person for him to see now that he was out of bed.

His memory of Auntie Julie began with conflict. When he was either four or five, Auntie Julie came to visit one day, and while Ma and Bendic talked with another visitor in the parlor, Auntie Julie jostled the children into the kitchen to interrogate them about what she said was their complete lack of respect. She shut the door behind her and right away asked, "Why do you people call your father by his name?" At first no one moved to answer. She scanned their faces disapprovingly and then focused on Paul's. "You cannot answer me?"

"Our father's name is Benedict," Bibi offered. "We, we call him Bendic, and—"

Auntie Julie cut her off. "What is the difference?" she asked, but didn't wait to get an answer. "You children have no fear at all. I see the easy hand with which your parents are raising you."

"Bendic hasn't complained about it," Paul began slowly, "and that's what we have always called him."

"Paul!" Auntie Julie shot back. "Don't you have any sense? You are the eldest, yet you cannot set a good example. I don't know what your mother teaches you. A man like your father, look at his age, look at you. Can't you see that he is old enough to be your grandfather?" She paused and pouted. "Okay, that aside, a big man like your father, don't you see how other people greet him? Yet you open your mouth and call him Bendic, Bendic, Bendic. Don't you hear what other children call their fathers?"

At this point Ajie was fed up and hoped Bibi would say something out of turn, blurt out words in exasperation, but she didn't.

"If you want to be respectful children," Auntie Julie continued, "you must call him Daddy, Papa, Pa. Choose one, but this Bendic rubbish must stop. Today!"

She looked at Paul to see if the matter could be left there, if he could be trusted this time to enforce the new rule. She stood over them and their little eyes flashed back at her: three tadpoles and one big fish. Auntie Julie called Bendic "sir," Ismaila the gateman and Marcus the driver both called Bendic "Oga," as they should, because he was their boss. Ma called him Ben, or Benedict sometimes. But the children called him Bendic. Ma said one day when Paul was about two, their father came in from work, and Paul jumped to his feet and called him "Bendic." Bendic and Ma were so happy that their formerly taciturn son had eventually found his tongue, they cooed the word back at him, encouraging him to say it again and again, and the name stuck. Bibi and Ajie took it up when they came along.

For some reason, Ajie's resentment of Auntie Julie sharpened that morning as he walked through the kitchen to the back of the house, where Bibi was sitting on the septic tank.

What sort of person, Ajie thought as he turned the doorknob that led to the backyard, would think giving their father an endearing name was equal to taking away the respect that was due him? What sort of person would force them to call their father *Daddy,* like all those silly children at school with their stupid plastic cartoon lunch boxes? It riled him even to think that someone like Auntie Julie could survive, was allowed to survive, in a world where his own brother could go missing for days.

That afternoon, when Auntie Julie had cornered them in the kitchen, they had all nodded, but her request was denied, firmly, silently. There was no Daddy, Pa, or Papa in their mouths. She mistook their silence for acquiescence; she rubbed their heads and pulled their little forms close in a kind of embrace, smothering their faces against her wrapper, her squishing blouse. The heavily sequined wrapper tied on her waist felt lukewarm on Ajie's cheeks. The smell of camphor (common with clothes left for too long at the bottom of a trunk) made Ajie feel malarial, sick enough to turn out his bowels in a feverish bout. He held his breath, counting and waiting for the embrace to end. He was on four and a half when she finally let go and he stood on his own feet. He looked down and saw her feet: the open front of her high-heeled sandals, the chipped red polish on her big toenails.

When Ajie opened the back door, he could hear Auntie Julie talking to Ismaila as she left. Bibi was sitting on the concrete slab of the soakway, with her back to the house, looking over at the neighbors' compound. The mango tree by the fence was thickly green with leaves but was without fruits.

"Bibi," he said as he came down the steps, "Bibi."

Bibi did not respond.

"You mean he didn't say anything at all before he left?" she asked without turning her back. "He must have said something to you."

Ajie stopped dead in his tracks, and guilt rose like tide-water up to his chest and made breathing very difficult. If anyone could have spared Paul from going missing, it should have been him.

CHAPTER THREE

P aul was four years old when Ajie was born. He often told Ajie that he remembered the day, a blazing hot Friday afternoon right after school. He also said Ajie was as black as charcoal at birth, and had a pair of bright red ears. Ajie had his doubts about this story but didn't contradict his brother. Instead, he would ask if Paul could remember the day Bibi was born. Was Paul not already two years old then? Were her ears also red? How tiny was her nose? If Bibi was within earshot, Ajie might rephrase the last question or withdraw it (Bibi hated her nose, and Ajie felt that with the way the thing was shaped, no one could blame her). If he was feeling ready for trouble, he would go ahead and ask whatever he wanted.

Bibi was not one to let things lie. She didn't rush into her battles, either; she courted them with a firm, steady hand. She would first allow her temper to heat up to the degree necessary. "I am warning you now," she would say, wagging a finger at Ajie, "stop that nonsense." She would fling him some bait, initiating a countdown. "One . . ." she would say in a level voice, then fold her arms across her chest and look away.

Once the count had begun, Ajie would find it impossible to resist.

"That is the problem you have, Ajie," Paul would say as a way of cautioning him, "you don't listen."

Ajie would find himself grinning. "Minus joke, Paul," he

would continue. "Okay, let's just say her nose was not tiny, then . . ."

"Two?" Bibi would curve it like a question.

". . . did her eyes close Chinese-style every time she tried to laugh?"

"Three!"

Bibi would unleash her rage like a whirlwind. Ajie would feel her transform in a flash, twirling and spinning toward him. He would yell, "Cool down! What did I—"

A slap. A knock on the head. Before he could recover from the shock of her assault, she would hold his lips together in a tight pinch, and Ajie would slap at her skinny arms. She would hold firm. A small ridge would form between her eyebrows as she pulled and twisted his lips. "You. Have. No. Respect! You. Have. No. Respect!" Ajie would kick at her and she would let go. Some days he gave slap for slap. If she grabbed him by the collar, he grabbed back, and the veins on their necks would stand out like tiny ropes. Paul would roll up an old magazine to hit them with. "Let go. Let go." They would dance about until Bibi did her swing—that was her winning move—putting all her weight on one leg, then hurling Ajie, with all her might, across the room. He would fly off, and with his own solid grip on her, she would follow and land on top of him, where it would be left to her to hit and hit. Then Paul would hold her hands and shout, "Bibi!," dragging her off. Panting heavily, righting her dress, she would snap her fingers at Ajie. "Try me next time."

"There is nothing you can do!" Ajie would yell back, his ears and cheeks stinging hot with pain.

"Enough is enough!" Paul"s voice would sound grave enough to silence them, at least for a while. They would wait for Bendic to return from work before reporting the case, because Ma had a hurried way of dealing with their disputes that wasn't worth the trouble. "How can you make fun of your older sister like that?" Ma would cut in. "My friend, let me not hear this next time." And then, turning to Bibi, "Don't you have any shame? You shouldn't be fighting your younger brother. The two of you, apologize." Bibi would wait for Ajie to go first. Ajie would wait, too, and then Ma would look at the two of them. "I'm not hearing anything, or have I gone deaf? Ajie, you are younger, go first."

Bendic was more thorough. Ajie would give his version of what happened, then Bibi would give hers, after which Paul would be called in as independent witness. If the stories contradicted each other, as they often did, Bendic would ask if there were parts of their accounts they wished to amend. It was a slow and thorough, courtlike process, but at the end, Bendic always found out who started the provocation. You reported a fight to Bendic only when you wanted your adversary singled out and punished, then yourself vindicated. But there you were, standing, trying to hold on to an aggravation that had long since disappeared. Blinking like a wall gecko.

"So why didn't you wait to report this, Bibi? Instead, you took laws into your hands and attacked your brother."

"But he looked for my trouble first."

"Where did you keep it?"

"What?"

"Your trouble, where did you keep it?"

Ajie could see the heat Bibi was coming under and hid his smile, looked down and held his hands together. Too much happiness can make you uncomfortable.

"Are you saying you can't control your anger?"

"I can," Bibi answered, her face thorny, like an open sack of nails. Her eyes reddened and began to fill up.

Then it was Ajie's turn, and you could easily see Bibi unknot as his motives were interrogated. The hem of her pinafore lifted and danced a little as she moved her weight from one foot to the other.

Even Paul never got off easy when he was a witness to a fight. "So, Paul," Bendic would say, now a bit weary but resolute, "you think it's fine to stand by and watch as your siblings pummel each other to death?"

"No, sir."

"Then what? Was there nothing you could have done to stop this silly argument from resulting in a fight?"

A long silence followed.

"Are you deaf, Paul? Or am I not speaking loudly enough for you?" The doors creaked at the harshness of Bendic's voice, and the parlor filled up with smoke.

Ajie could feel the blood pounding inside Paul's head, the mad beating of his temples, and the roaring going on inside him: *I didn't do anything! It's not my fault!*

Bendic restrained his anger, reined it in with a deep breath, his voice mellowed. "Okay, explain yourself."

"It was supposed to be a joke, but Bibi wasn't finding it funny, and she warned Ajie to stop. Ajie didn't, so she tried to make him."

"Make him what?"

"Make him stop, maybe."

"How?"

"I'm not sure. She grabbed his neck."

"She grabbed his neck," Bendic echoed. "And you sat and watched?"

No answer.

"Yes or no?"

"Well, yes. I tried to stop them, but I wasn't quick enough."

"I've said it many times in this house, that you are responsible for the actions you take as well as the actions you should—or could—have taken but didn't. What would have happened if you had injured yourselves in the process?" Bendic continued. "You think your mother and I would be happy to find you wounded or constantly replacing torn clothes? You think this is what we like to return home to every day?"

One particular evening while they were having an after-fight session, Paul walked over to where the clothes were lying on the floor—a pile of evidence—between where they stood and where Bendic sat in the puffed leather chair in his study, and picked up the clothes. "I will mend them," he said.

Paul was able to do this type of thing. He could muster the courage and take the initiative, and it would seem natural—like this was what people did or were supposed to do: They stepped forward before judgment was passed on them; they accepted the blame and decided all by themselves what amends they would make.

Ajie tried to copy this code once, and it backfired. He had broken a new boy's pencil at school by accident, and the boy had gone to complain to the teacher. When Ajie was summoned and interrogated, he told the teacher that it was an accident, he was sorry and planned to replace the pencil the next day. The teacher looked him up and down and asked who he thought he was to talk like that. "You go about destroying people's property and then tell them you can replace it? Ajie Utu!" She reached down for her cane, asked Ajie to stretch out his hand, and delivered three stern strokes. His school report at the end of that term said, "Should learn to respect the property of fellow pupils."

In the year Bibi turned nine and Ajie seven, their fighting stopped. Bendic, working on what he said was a very serious case, had come home straight from court and witnessed the final stages of a major brawl. The living room furniture was in disarray, books scattered about the floor, slippers came slicing through the air. Bendic's voice boomed from where he stood by the door and knocked the fight out of them. Ajie had scratches all over his face; Bibi had a bruised lower lip.

"It will never happen again," was how Bendic put it. "Not in this house . . . to return and hear that there has been a fight." He didn't let anyone take his briefcase from him, or the black gown held in the crook of his arm. He stood there in the middle of the mess they had made. "You are both old enough to resolve your differences without having to resort to blows." There was no room for courtroom dramas that day, no careful interrogation and weighing of actions. Bendic was fed up with the fighting and simply outlawed it.

Ajie and Bibi never fought each other again, at least not in their usual physical ways. They invented other methods of combat.

Ajie, however, carried on fighting at school. Twice that term, at least. Nnaemeka Anigwe, an overweight boy with breasts, knocked the biscuit out of Ajie's hand during break time and ran off with it. Ajie chased after the boy, tripped him, and they both crashed on the ground. They struggled. Ajie tried to pry the boy's mouth open to force out the brown mash, but he bared his teeth and swallowed again and again, determined to seal his victory. *So now what?* Ajie wondered. Was he to let this boy get up, dust himself off, and walk?

Then there was Lara Gasper, who pointed at him one afternoon, covering her nose with her other hand, and then told the class he had farted. All eyes turned to Ajie. He hadn't even been aware anyone had farted. And now that all of Primary 3B was looking at him, should he glare about in clear-conscience surprise and say, "No, I didn't fart," "It wasn't me"? Or yield his rear for them to sniff his shorts? Ajie was still pondering his options. He didn't know when he slapped Lara hard across the face. He simply heard the sharp ring of the slap and the dead silence that followed, as if every other sound had been sucked out of the classroom. He looked around and saw the gasping students, the shock on Lara's face, and realized what he had done. He stilled himself from an instant show of regret. Why should she go about bearing false witness? he thought. Lara grabbed his shirt and rained some quick slaps on his chest, but her eyes were brimming, so she ran off to complain. The teacher, Mr. Dike, made him face the wall, kneel down, raise his hands, and apologize after he had spent all of the free period on his knees. Ajie felt sorry and did apologize, but the stupid girl, Lara, said she couldn't quite hear him. "Audible!" Mr. Dike bellowed from the back. "I said, be audible!" So Ajie said the words again, this time loud and slow. *"I am very sorry, Lara. I will never, ever do that to you again or to anybody else."*

As he walked back to his seat, he wondered if this incident would get into his end-of-term report. He imagined the hurt in Bendic's eyes. *You hit a fellow pupil, what are you turning into? Right under my roof.* Bendic's disappointment, anger, and concern all rolled into that unreadable, serene quality that could be mistaken for leniency. Ajie resigned himself to fate. The worst could happen: Bendic would hear of his misconduct and then use him as an example for his siblings. He might flog Ajie (something he had never done), or he might stop paying his school fees, send the money to a child in the village or one of those boys who hawked meat pie and bread on Aba Road; a child who, because of what he had suffered, would better appreciate a good education and show some gratitude for it. *My hands are tied,* Ajie imagined Bendic saying, *but this is the only way you can learn.*

For the whole of that afternoon, through social studies lesson and composition exercise, Ajie planned his defense. He would beg. He would plead momentary anger; it wasn't really a fight, he didn't know when it happened, he lost his temper, the slap slipped out of him, and there was no way to take it back. *Give me one more chance, please, Bendic.*

Years later, in boarding school, when Ajie fought again, it was with proper blows, kicks, and tumbles in a rough circle of cheering boys in shorts and checked gingham shirts. He couldn't recall all the details of this fight. He remembered the boy, whose father, it turned out, died later that term in a car crash on the Lagos-Ibadan Expressway. He could not remember what led to the fight.

After Bendic walked in on Ajie and Bibi's skirmish and outlawed fighting in the house, he dropped his briefcase on the dining table and walked into his room. No one spoke or moved for a while, and the house settled into a deep silence and near-evening shadows. The power outage had stretched for hours. Their parents' bedroom door was left wide open for air. Bendic was taking a nap, lying almost spread-eagled on the king-size bed. The curtains were hiked up and tucked in severely on the rails, the French windows pushed out so that the room was filled with the waning afternoon light. Paul walked along the passage on the balls of his feet. He turned the doorknob to his and Ajie's room, slowly, to suppress the click. Ajie followed in slow motion, stepping high on his toes. Paul pulled out the side drawer by his bed and got out a comic book he had borrowed from Fola, slim and glossy, with speech balloons floating about the front page. He rolled up the book and put it in his pocket, though most of it stuck out on the side of his T-shirt.

"Let's go."

"I'm coming," Ajie said, changing quickly into a fresh T-shirt.

"What's Bibi doing?"

"I don't know." He didn't care.

Fola's father was not back from work when they got to his house. "Let's go to the back," Fola said after he met them near the gate, "my mother is with a visitor."

Paul handed him the comic book.

"I have others. I went to Leventis with my father on Saturday. I got four more," Fola said.

"Ask me a capital," Ajie interjected as they walked past the septic tanks. After the afternoon's ordeal with Bendic, he was determined to lighten his own mood.

"State or country?" Paul asked.

Fola's house help must have spent the morning washing bedsheets and towels. They ducked their heads under the line sagging with clothes long dried. Two blue pillowcases and something with bold stripes had fallen to the ground, crisp.

"States are easy," Ajie said. "I have the highest score in my class in general knowledge."

"If you want to do something difficult," Fola said, "try the thirteen times table."

"We do fourteen times tables first thing every morning now," Paul said. "Our new teacher is Ghanaian. He is very serious. If he catches you hesitating or chewing your lip, he"ll single you out to recite it in front of the class. Olumide got six strokes today for getting three answers wrong."

"Ask me any country's capital and I will tell you," Ajie said, bringing them back to where they started.

"Namibia."

"Windhoek," Ajie answered.

"I just gave you an easy one. Wait, let me think." Fola paused. "Mmm . . . El Salvador."

"San Salvador."

"Suriname?" Paul asked this time.

"What?" Fola made a sound between mockery and surprise. "Is that even a country? Okay, answer that."

Ajie stood still, eyes distant, moving his lips a little as if muttering to himself.

"You don't know it!" Fola chirped.

"Paramaribo," Ajie exclaimed, and then walked on.

"Did he get it?" Fola asked, looking at Paul.

Paul nodded. "Good one."

"Another?"

"Iceland," Fola said, distracted.

"Reykjavík." The answer came before Fola finished.

"Is that how to pronounce it?"

"Rei-ka-vik. And I can spell it if you want."

"Let's do something else, please," Fola said, unable to suppress his boredom.

Behind Fola's house was a sloping field cut to a low brush. A small house that was formerly the servants' quarters stood at the corner by the fence. They sat by the barbed wire fence that separated the house from the mangrove creek where flying insects appeared all at once. The boys flapped their hands in the air and slapped some against their bodies.

Paul stood up and walked toward the mango tree by the fence. He jumped up, caught a branch, and clambered up the tree.

"Our gateman killed a snake from that tree last week," Fola said apprehensively. "He was shaking it for ripe mangoes and a big snake fell down."

"Really!" Paul said with wide eyes, looking down at Fola from the tree.

"I'm serious," Fola said, sounding ominous, as though a slither of snakes might just descend upon them at any moment.

"What color was the snake?" Ajie asked.

"What?"

"The snake your gateman killed, what color was it?"

"Green."

Paul had jumped down from the tree, rubbing tree bark from his arms. "How long was the snake?" he asked.

"As long as this." Fola stretched out his right hand, and then with his other hand, he picked a region near the center of his chest. "Or even longer. Our gateman buried it right there." He pointed at a spot near the fence.

"It's probably a tree snake," Paul said after a while.

Ajie knew then that Paul would be going up the tree anyway.

"You know tree snakes don't bite," Paul said, looking at Fola. "You said it was green, right?" He was engaging his expertise on snakes, an expertise gained solely by looking through Ma's encyclopedias and watching the occasional wildlife documentary on TV.

"Hmm, I don't know for you-o, Paul," Fola said.

Ajie wanted to note that its color and placement in a tree weren't enough facts to determine that it was the venomless tree snake. He knew Paul wanted to climb the tree, so he stayed silent. His mind was changing by the second: Maybe Paul was right and it was just an ordinary tree snake.

Paul was climbing up the tree. Ajie watched as he moved from branch to branch. Soon he was at the very top. He stood on a branch and began to reach out for the fruits. He didn't ask either Ajie or Fola to join. Just being up there seemed a strong enough invitation.

He sank his teeth into a mango. "Should I throw some down for you?"

"I'm coming up," Fola said.

"Me, too."

Ajie stood up and began pulling himself up the trunk of the tree, upward, upward, inch by inch, till he got to the first spread of branches and caught hold of one, then hauled his body up the tree. "If you are afraid, you will fall," Paul said, looking down at Ajie. "You are not heavy enough to break a branch, just hold tight."

Ajie could see Paul's gray T-shirt up there with the green leaves and blue sky. Fola was right beneath him now, on the same branch, his breath heavy and labored. A stiff wind blew through and rustled the leaves, and Ajie's heart skipped a beat, but he laughed out, "Wow!" On the treetop, they perched on the youngest branches like three little birds, looking down on all the rooftops from here to the expressway, watching cars come and go but without hearing the engines.

"If we climb down to the branch below," Paul said, "we can jump to the other side of the fence."

Another gust, stronger than the first, blew and whispered

past Ajie's ears, and he imagined being caught on the barbed wire while trying to jump. He held on tight to the branch beside him and looked across the desiccating swamp, catching a whiff of the muddy stink, imagining his exhilaration at having jumped. It was the present notion of actually doing it that knotted his lungs and made breathing difficult.

Fola was quiet. Ajie wanted him to say something, to discourage his brother. He knew that once Paul jumped, he, too, would have to.

"How do we get back?" Ajie asked.

"We'll walk all the way around to the gate," Paul said. He was tapping his foot on a branch, testing its strength to see if it could withstand his takeoff. He must have judged it could: He took off and landed on the other side with a muted thud. "It's easy!"

Fola went next. He inched forward and misstepped on the branch but held on tight and kept steady for some seconds. His jump was sharp and quick. When he landed, he got up at once and hopped on one foot. Ajie looked beyond the rooftops and slow-moving cars in the distance, all suddenly small as though he were on an airplane. *What will it be, then,* Ajie thought. He tried to imagine the near future, that evening back in their house, for instance, would it have already happened that he made the jump, feeling proud that he had pushed himself and done it, or would he be nursing his disgrace and cowardice at having chickened out? Would it have happened that he climbed down the tree and walked through the gate to join Paul and Fola on the other side?

"Ajie!" Paul shouted from below. "I'm here, nothing will happen to you."

Ajie took off without thinking. There was only the slap of

wind against his face and nothing else. A quick blur of green, blue, brown. When he landed on the other side, first on his feet, followed by a backward fall on his bottom, Paul pulled him up by the hand.

"Champion. You see, you made it!" Ajie dusted his shorts as they made their way back. Paul dropped a hand on his shoulder.

They walked all the way around to the street, just in time to meet Bibi at Fola's gate.

"They are looking for you people," she said, looking only at Paul. "Uncle Gabby is around." Fola said goodbye and went back into his compound as Paul, Bibi, and Ajie walked back home.

A white van was parked in their driveway. "Is Mr. Ifenwa here, too?" Paul asked.

"Maybe he's just come. He wasn't here when I left to find you."

Bendic was in his favorite seat, holding a beer mug in his left hand. "They are back!" he announced to the others. Gabby was sitting next to Bendic; he balanced a bottle of malt drink on his lap. Bendic's friend Mr. Ifenwa was perched on the edge of his seat, leaning toward a saucer of groundnuts he was shelling and throwing into his mouth.

"Where did you two escape to?" Bendic asked, almost as if addressing the whole room. They greeted him and Mr. Ifenwa, and Paul stood behind their uncle Gabby. Gabby was Ma's young cousin. He had lived with them once for about a year, while preparing for his O levels, and now that he was in university, he came down sometimes to spend weekends with them.

"I think you have grown taller since the last time I saw you," Mr. Ifenwa said. "No, I mean you." He gestured toward Ajie, then emptied the contents of a groundnut pod into his mouth. *Not true,* Ajie thought. It was Paul who always grew taller. Visitors never failed to comment on it. To Ajie they said things like: *So, what class are you in now? Already? Wonderful. What do you want to be when you grow up? A lawyer like your father?*

"Lawyers are liars," Mr. Ifenwa sometimes said. "Let the boy study what he wants, when the time comes."

"There was a bank robbery near Eleme Junction," Gabby was saying now. "I heard it on the bus as I was coming."

"You don't say," said Ma.

"The operation lasted a good two hours; the police were nowhere."

The remote control was resting on the arm of Ma's chair, and Bibi took it without her noticing, then flipped back and forth between the two channels. She would pause for a few seconds on one and then the other. Ajie saw that Paul was conversing with Gabby in hushed tones. He was trying to get Gabby out of his seat to the dining area, where they could talk freely.

Gabby, the connoisseur of ghost stories. ("Last week, when I was on my way to visit a friend near Wimpey, the taxi driver picked up a woman by the cemetery near Hospital Junction; each time the driver looked in his rearview mirror, he saw a coffin where this woman sat. He would turn his head only to find the woman on her seat, smiling meekly at him. His eyes went up to the rearview mirror, then back to the woman. At the third glance, he stopped the car in panic and ran out, shouting, 'Jesus! Jesus!' We looked and the woman had vanished, leaving a white hankie behind.")

Gabby, master of high farce. ("A heavily pregnant woman was knocked down by a bus as she tried to cross the road at Rumuola. As the car hit her, the child—a boy—evacuated her womb at once and made his way straight into GRA via Presidential Hotel. The police are in full search for him right now, as we speak.")

A thin, shiny scar ran across Gabby's scalp, just above his left earlobe, which confirmed him as a man who frequently had dangerous encounters. Gabby had come down to Port Harcourt from the village to sit for his WASC exams. This was in 1984, when the military regime had imposed a nine P.M. curfew. Gabby was walking home from his evening preparatory lessons when the police stopped him. "Come here, who are you, do you have any ID on you, where are you coming from, where are you going," and Gabby answered these questions, he was only a few minutes' walk home, there was more than enough time before the curfew began. "Wait here," one of the policemen ordered, then ignored him until it was nine P.M.

"Are you not aware there is a curfew from nine?" the policeman returned to ask Gabby. "What is it by your time now?" Gabby couldn't help laughing. Was this man serious? Gabby couldn't imagine how to react to the scene unfolding before him, so he laughed again as the policeman made a show of the gravity of Gabby's offense.

"Oh, you are laughing, eh?" the policeman charged. "I will show you today."

"Just let me go home, I beg you," Gabby said, gesturing to the nearby street, but the policeman kept him there for another hour and then told him he was being arrested for breaking the curfew. He radioed his colleagues for a van, which they pushed Gabby into. He was being driven to the station for questioning, they said. By the time he was released the next morning, they had somehow managed to break his head in the process of interrogation.

Bibi had joined Paul and Gabby at the dining table. "I can set the tennis board if you like," Paul said to Gabby. "This time you won't even get up to ten points before I trash you. I can give you five to start with." Gabby had beaten Paul at table tennis during his last visit, months ago. "Or do you want ten points to start off with? I can give you that, don't be afraid. Get up."

"It's late," Ma said, her attention swinging from Bendic's conversation with Mr. Ifenwa to Paul's. "Gabby is tired."

"Tomorrow, Paul," said Gabby.

"Ohhh," the children groaned.

"I'm sure Ajie can beat you. Even with his left hand, his loop is something else," Paul said. "And he stands on a tire to play."

"That's because he is a dwarf," Bibi said.

Even though Ajie didn't particularly mind that she had said that, he waited for an opportunity in the conversation that would allow him deliver a sharp retort.

Mr. Ifenwa poured his Guinness into a large mug and placed the bottle back on the table with a gentle thud. He clinked glasses with Bendic, who was browsing through a magazine. "Ah, thank you, my sister," Mr. Ifenwa said to Ma after taking a sip of the cold drink. "This is what someone needs on a day like this."

Ma smiled and waved him off. "Thank me for what?" she said, as any gracious host would.

"How do you get your drinks so cold with NEPA and their manic power cuts?" Mr. Ifenwa asked.

"We are supposed to get power every other day, but sometimes we don't see any light for three days in a row. We have to run the generator to keep our food from going bad," Ma said.

"It's wonderful," Mr. Ifenwa said, but it was unclear if he meant the cold beer or the constant power cuts.

"Ifenwa, so how are you getting on with your school?" Bendic asked. "Have any students enrolled yet?"

"Nearly fifteen," he replied with a glow of pride.

"Really?" Ma said, her voice a little louder. "Where did you find them?"

"I recruit from everywhere," Mr. Ifenwa said, scratching his head and then straightening up. "Some are my neighbors. You know those mechanics by the junction to my house? Two of them have joined."

"You don't say," Bendic's voice was barely louder than a mumble; his eyes traced the magazine left to right and back.

"Have you given it a name yet?" Ma asked. Mr. Ifenwa shook his head.

"Ifenwa School of Adult Education," Bendic suggested without missing a beat.

"Spoken like a true bourgeois," Mr. Ifenwa responded, about to smile. "Why must it have my name?" Then the almost-smile disappeared.

Bendic and Mr. Ifenwa were schoolmates and had become so deft at sparring in this way that you had to listen hard to catch that it was only amicable rivalry. Mr. Ifenwa wore egg-shaped lenses with thin silver frames that looked transparent. He used to live in America with his wife, Celia. They had returned to Nigeria one December for the holiday when Celia was killed in a car crash as they drove from their home village, Nnobi, to Port Harcourt. A broken-down trailer had been abandoned by a bend in the road without any warning signs to oncoming vehicles. She slipped away before they got to the hospital, and Mr. Ifenwa never returned to America. Although Ajie had never heard Mr. Ifenwa and his parents discuss his dead wife, and even before Ajie grew to know the story, it never left him—the death of his wife. It was an old musty smell of a cupboard seldom opened. His two sons still lived in America. One taught at a college in Boston, the other did something at a medical research center.

Now Bendic was saying something to Ma that Ajie hadn't heard. Bibi skipped off from the dining area and hurried out of the parlor. She returned with Paul's Walkman with the headset on, nodding a little as she listened, walking toward Paul's outstretched hand. Paul took the tape out, turned it over, and put on the earphones. He listened for a few seconds to make sure it was the song he wanted before passing it to Gabby, watching his face for a reaction as he put it on and listened.

Ma took the remote control and flipped the channel, and there was Georgie Gold, a flamboyant local singer who wore her hair in a startling blonde, swinging her hips this way and that in her heavily sequined dress, belting out a tune Ma apparently didn't care for. Ma seemed frustrated by the lack of choice on TV, but she may not have realized it, as Ajie watched her drop the remote control back on the arm of her chair in weary surrender. Ajie went to the dining area, where Gabby was telling Paul and Bibi a fantastical story about a village he once drove past. It was a land of only women. They never grew old.

"Oh, Benedict, you can do better than that." Mr. Ifenwa's voice came from across the room. Bendic responded: "We can get opinions by the dozen, but I want the facts. Give me something research based, then I will listen."

Ajie knew they were having yet another argument. Sometimes Bendic called Mr. Ifenwa a "Communist," and he called Bendic a "decadent bourgeois." When Bendic said the military had brought Nigeria to its lowest point yet in history, Mr. Ifenwa would add that direct action was the only way out. In

Mr. Ifenwa's opinion, Nigeria was comatose, nailed shut in a coffin slowly moving toward a furnace.

After Celia died, Mr. Ifenwa spent the following years as a one-man campaigner for road safety: He wrote letters to the ministry of Works and Transport, he wrote articles that were published in the *Tide* newspaper and sometimes the national *Punch*. Many times he pinned placards on his body and stood before the Federal Secretariat. He had abandoned his job in the U.S., and even though his children pleaded with him many times to return, he didn't. Two months earlier he had started a school for adult education. "The number of people I meet who have been to primary school but can't read well is just alarming," he had said.

"What about school fees?" Ma was asking now. "Are you charging yet?

"Not yet, my sister."

"We can brainstorm, think up a suitable name. It's really admirable, this idea. No joke, you must give me some advisory role in it," Bendic said.

Mr. Ifenwa said, "There is no money to share here, Ben."

"Me? Ifenwa." Bendic was perched on the edge of his seat, pointing his fingers at his own chest. "Me, share money?" He shook his head and laughed like a bad man in a film. "I have suffered. Anyway, my dear friend," he continued, "when you do decide on a name, avoid anything that has *People, Masses,* or *Common Man.*"

"It is cynicism that has kept the country in this state, Benedict."

"I'm just saying, coming from you, it would be a bit of a cliché, don't you think? It could only be worse if you gave it a Pentecostal Christian name, like, say . . . El-Shaddai Cradle of Learning," and they burst into laughter.

"Or Divine Grace Group of Schools," Ma added.

Mr. Ifenwa piped up. "I'm thinking of a name like No Condition Is Permanent. The ethos is clear enough. Anyone, regardless of current literacy level, can come and change for the better."

"I know, I know," Bendic said. "But that phrase is written on every bus or truck plying Aba Road."

"And that's exactly why it's the right name: nonexclusive."

"Hmm, I see your point," Bendic mused. "It might work. In fact, I think it will work," he said with certainty.

"Ol' boy," Mr. Ifenwa's voice dipped from that cultured mix that had as much of Igbo in it as English, "so the name don win you over!" His English was of a kind that Ajie recognized only in people of his parents' generation. They said *perhaps* instead of *maybe*. *Peradventure* was a word that occurred in regular conversations. Ajie was with Ma one day at Savannah Bank, and Ma told him to sit in the lobby while she went inside to speak to her banker. Ajie overheard a woman say, "Good a thing the government paid us when they did." He turned his head to find the owner of the voice, and there she was, standing with three other women who might have been ex-colleagues. "If not that one has children who are able to augment one's pension . . ." She let the words trail off like someone reluctant to show off her own good fortune. The four women kept vigilante eyes on what was going on at the front of the line. Pensioner types who probably ran into each other only monthly at the bank or whenever their payments came through. Although the woman Ajie heard speaking looked better dressed than the others, there was an austere neatness to her. Her skirt and blouse were made from reddish Ankara print; she wore Scholl slippers on her feet. Slung on her left shoulder was a puffy handbag from which the black head of a small umbrella stuck out. Her hair was evenly gray, freshly combed, tightly curled, and gleaming. When the fluorescent tube right above began to blink, for a moment her hair looked like a dark halo around her face. Ajie couldn't make up his mind if she looked dignified, or poor, or both.

"So you are not charging any fees at your school?" Ma asked Mr. Ifenwa.

"I will charge for study materials, but not yet. For now I need to encourage people to enroll. The notebooks and stationery you sent will go a long way."

Ma stood up, collected the empty bottles from the table, and went into the kitchen.

Bendic turned on the television and asked Mr. Ifenwa if he'd read a particular story in the *Vanguard*. It was about a director in the Ministry of Education who'd claimed there were no funds to pay pensioners for the past three months, but there were now allegations that he had put the money on a fixed deposit to make interest on it, and yesterday a large crowd of pensioners gathered in front of his office at the state secretariat, demanding to be paid at once.

Two local schools were dueling on a debate program on TV. Baptist High and Oromineke Girls. The topic was juvenile delinquency: Who was to blame, the parents or the school? The studio audience members were mostly students from both schools, seated on opposite sides. The students from Oromineke Girls were dressed in checked green uniforms, and the Baptist boys wore white shirts and white trousers. The panel was seated at the center.

A girl in a neatly pressed green checked dress opposed the notion that the schools were to blame. She spoke fast. The words rushed out of her and Ajie's mind raced behind, grasping them when she was already on to the next sentence. Her hands flew up now and again. Finally, she turned with alacrity toward the rival school and said with defiance, "I hope with these few points of mine, I have been able to convince my opponents that . . ." A storm of clapping followed when she finished. The moderator called for the second speaker from Baptist High. A boy in white trousers and a long-sleeved shirt moved to the center.

"He looks a little bit like Paul," Ma said.

"No way," Paul said.

"He does," Ma insisted. "You just can't see it. Look at his nose and forehead."

"I don't agree."

"Keep arguing."

"Paul will be taller when he gets to that age," Gabby said.

"Let's hear what the boy is saying, at least," Bendic grunted.

"Moderator," the boy began, motioning with a sweep of his hand, "panel of impartial judges, co-debater, accurate time-keepers, viewers at home, good day." His voice was steady and strong, the cadence of rehearsed thoughtfulness. "I am here to propose the motion that juvenile delinquency is primarily caused by the home. My erring opponent has said—"

The entire parlor disappeared into blackness. The TV went dead. "NEPA!" someone gasped. "Oooh!" the children moaned. "What kind of nonsense is this?"

"Bendic, should I ask Ismaila if there is any diesel?" Paul asked, his shadow by the door, ready to leave. Ma's slippers flapped in the kitchen. Then there was the sound of a match being struck and the flash of flame. She placed the lantern on the dining table and trimmed the light to the desired brightness.

"While we wait," Ma said. It was a moving-on kind of voice.

While we wait for power to be restored so we can return—if we are lucky—to the tail end of this debate we were just beginning to enjoy. While we wait, here is a lantern.

"So long as the power situation is not solved in this country," Mr. Ifenwa said, "we are going nowhere."

The metal railings on the veranda rattled. Paul's voice: "Ismaila said the fuel can carry for some hours."

"Okay, let him put it on. Maybe for an hour. Let's finish the program, at least."

"He should watch out," Ma added, "for when NEPA returns light so he can switch over."

They caught the last fifteen minutes of the show. The boy (who may or may not have looked like Paul) was finishing his argument. "Thank you," he said firmly, then turned around to take his seat as clapping broke out yet again.

Years later, Ajie would remember this particular debate. He would also remember Paul's picture coming up on TV, on the two stations in the city, as announcements of his disappearance were being made. Five days after Paul disappeared, Bendic went to the TV stations with Paul's photograph. He provided them with Paul's full name, his age, when and where he was last seen, and then there was an appeal for any information that might aid in finding him. By now their earlier feelings of discord between hope and fear had fallen away, and there were just horror and dread. Ajie would remember the boy TV debater and would mix up his face with Paul's. He would replace Paul's clothes with this boy's white and white. It would make perfect sense to him, because at the time of the disappearance, Paul was about this boy's age, only a little taller.

CHAPTER FOUR

The seeds of Paul's disappearance were sowed by his parents. This was what Ajie decided. And who else was there to blame? Not Bibi, she had no hand in the matter. As for Paul, you really can't blame a person for his own disappearance, at least not while he is still missing and cannot speak for himself.

To tell Paul's story, you would have to start from before he was born. The life of Bendic and Ma together was well documented in the framed photographs hanging on the walls of their village home in Ogibah. A house that took five years to build and was finally completed the year Bibi was born. Ma and Bendic were arrayed in various settings in these pictures. The backdrops were wrought-iron gates of colleges in the newly independent Nigeria, stone monuments in gray English cities; they were smiling and holding hands in a pigeon-littered square in Rome, standing with flutes of champagne in their hands at a party in Port Harcourt, leaning on a white Volkswagen Igala on a side street in Lagos.

They returned from England in '64 and took up civil service jobs in Lagos: Bendic in the Ministry of Justice, Ma in Education. Bendic was sporting a thick mustache, his dark-framed spectacles, and a dark suit. Ma was in a sleeveless shift dress and clunky heels. They both had buoyant Afros and wore bell-bottom trousers in the early pictures. Down the years, Ma's enormous hair softened into Jheri curls; Bendic's suits turned beige, and his hair was patted down, looking milder, less radical.

There were hundreds of photographs stored in the albums in the Formica sideboard. Bibi had this habit then. Each time they were in the Ogibah house, she would point someone out in a group photograph and ask, "Ma, who is this person?" and Ma would ask her to bring the photo closer. Sometimes the name came immediately, often with a side story. At other times Ma would go, "Mmm . . . is this not . . . ?" and Bendic would help out. Or they might decide it was a friend's friend they'd met at the dinner party.

In another photo they were in the foyer of the Cedar Palace Hotel; Bendic was wearing a lace tunic with embroidery around the neck and thick black-framed glasses.

"I think we had just been to the cinema," Bendic explained.

Ma's hair was tied up in a wrap; she was clutching a clasp purse under her arm, and her skirt was made of *aso-oke*, darkly striped and very short.

There was a studio photo in which Ma was sitting on a cane chair with a fancy mat spread underneath it. She was dressed in a loose flowered maxi gown, the hem of which rested on her ankle. Her legs were crossed, showing off clunky wooden heels, and next to her, standing on the mat, was Bendic, slender-hipped, in flared trousers and a patterned shirt; his long-collared shirt was undone three buttons down, revealing chest hair. His left hand was resting on Ma's shoulder. They wore serious faces and wide dark glasses. Ajie liked this picture more than all the others. It was his firm belief that this was what movie stars of those days looked like. One day he asked Bendic if he and Ma used to be actors, and Bendic answered, "What?" Like someone who hadn't heard the question, or maybe it was a silly question to ask. So Ajie turned around, brought the picture to Bendic, and pointed. "Look."

When their parents talked about their time in Lagos, their voices softened and they spoke as if it were another life altogether, more exciting than the one they had now. Paul, Bibi, and Ajie dubbed the period "Those Days in Lagos," because Ma always began stories with "Those days in Lagos . . ." Sometimes it happened when she came across a dress in her wardrobe or something in her trunk box—a purse, coral beads—that reminded her of the time. She would hold the item a little away from her face to get a better look. "Twenty-five Enitan, Ikeja, Lagos. Ah-ah," she would hiccup, as if there were someone there to disbelieve her. And without looking toward Bendic, she would say, "We lived life then, Ben." It was something like pride mixed with regret. The war had broken out after the eastern region announced secession from the rest of the country, and they had rushed back home to be close to family. Sometimes a prominent person's name would come up on the national news, and Ma would say they had known the person back then in Lagos. Was he not such-and-such person's husband? Or did she not work in the same office with this-and-that person? "We lost touch with so many good friends."

That same tone was in her voice one day at the market when she surprised the butcher, interrupting him with her own thundery Yoruba, to the man's surprise. The butcher had said to his assistant in Yoruba to give Ma a tough bargain, as she looked like she had a lot of money in her bag.

"*Ole Olodo,*" Ma fired out. "Stupid thief."

The man covered his mouth with his hands in mock wonder,

bleated out a nervous laugh, and cowered. "My sister," he begged in English, "it's not like that."

"How is it, then?" Ma shot back, giving him a mean look. Rather than condemn the butcher for trying to cheat her, she said to him instead in pidgin, "Nearly ten years I live for Lagos," as if the man's principal offense were his lack of discernment. She got a discount, and the man, with quick slashes of his knife, chopped up some more of the red meat and threw it all into the black cellophane bag for goodwill.

"You are my customer now-o, madam," he said, laughing.

"Na so." Ma was either unimpressed or feigning it. She gestured to Paul to pick up the bag, and they made their way toward the hub of women at the end of the market who operated large grinding machines where, at a small charge, you could get your tomatoes blended and the puree packaged securely in a cellophane bag.

Bibi pointed out a woman in the fish section and whispered to Ajie that the woman was an actress in a television drama. "Nchelem. Don't you know her? From *Willi-Willi . . . Hot Cash.*"

"It's not her," Ajie said, and looked in another direction to insist on his point.

"Stay out of the way," Ma said to the two of them. "Come this way." She pulled Ajie close as a shirtless, sweaty man pushed past them with a wheelbarrow loaded with sacks of onions. Paul handed the bag of fresh tomatoes to the woman behind the grinder, who started the noisy engine and then began yelling prices at Ma.

When they got back to the car, Ma said she had taught the butcher a lesson. She seemed pleased with her performance.

Paul said it didn't really matter; the man would cheat someone else who didn't understand the language.

"Egg zatly," Bibi said. Ajie sniffed, because Bibi always wanted to have some input in every discussion.

"That's his business if he doesn't want to learn," Ma insisted, bent on making a lesson for her children, "but at least this should show you can't always judge people at face value."

"Face value," Paul echoed, and Ajie wondered about Face Value as the car made its slow, bumpy exit out of Oroworukwo onto Aba Road, and as it climbed the low hillock at St. John's and descended toward the traffic lights at Garrison, where, to their right, scaffolding had gone up outside the Hotel Chez Therese, but there were no workmen about. On the island between the express lanes, in the traffic controller's booth, a madman in long brown dreads stood, frantically motioning to cars, and his enormous scrotum dangled and jiggled from the effort. The lights turned green and their car sped toward home, while Ajie still mulled over Face Value and the madman's morbidly enormous balls and the butcher's knife. Ma honked as they approached 11 Yakubu. Paul got out of the car to help Ismaila open the gate.

Paul was born in the year Bendic became a Christian; that was why they gave him the name. "After the apostle formerly known as Saul," Bibi would always say with glee, marveling at her own wit. It might be more accurate to refer to this period as the year Bendic renewed his Christian commitments. His father's being a churchman would have made it unlikely for Bendic to have escaped a Christian upbringing altogether.

Bendic was the sixth of eight boys and the only one to live past the age of nineteen. The others drowned, fell off a tree in those early days of timber trading, got bitten by a snake. One strong-headed one went to the farm on a sacred day of the bush and saw Erusumini the beautiful, the serpent goddess, glowing in the lonely afternoon light. He ran home and collapsed, hot with fever, then convulsed and died that same night, frothing at the mouth. The second set of twins weren't only drowned at birth; the man whose family duty it was to carry out the task—having great pity on the mother, who had now suffered the abomination twice—pierced the eyes of the boys as their lungs filled with water. He would blind them from seeing their way back to this same family to cause sorrow.

Everything that came to Bendic's parents through birth seemed shy of adulthood except Bendic. And by the time Bendic had his own children, he was old enough to be a grandfather.

In the years that followed Paul's birth, the years before Bibi and Ajie were born, Bendic's brief spiritual revival had mellowed, so he gave the two of them Ogba names that had nothing to do with God. He didn't bother with a Christian or English middle name, as was the fashion then among the educated classes.

On a cool March morning in 1978, Bendic got baptized at Idu waterside. His father had died a few weeks earlier, and Ma had just found out she was pregnant for the first time.

"The world is such a funny place," Ma would say later to her children, "my mother-in-law, your grandmother, would have been the happiest woman in the world to hear the news. But she was in her grave before her time. When I first realized I was pregnant and thought of how happy she would have been, it made me sad to know she had missed all of it."

The children knew little about Bendic's mother except that she died of heartbreak during the war. Bendic hardly ever spoke about it. Ma one day told them the story. She said it was unfair for them to ask their father.

An Ogibah man had gone to report to the Biafran authorities that Bendic was a saboteur, that he was a supporter of and a spy for the Nigeria side. It was nearly a year since the war began. There were rumors everywhere, about how Oguta had fallen, how Port Harcourt was soon to be captured. Prominent members of non-Igbo minorities were being seized and thrown into detention on suspicion of sabotage. Soldiers came one afternoon and arrested Bendic. They said they were taking him away for questioning, nothing to fear, if he was innocent he would be returned. Two days after they took him, Ma borrowed a bicycle and set out to look for him. Another Ogibah man, whom she said she would never forget, rode with her on the journey. His name was Ireju. They got to Ahoada, and the people there said the soldiers had carried the detainees to Elele. They got to Elele and were told they had moved them that afternoon to Isiokpo. At Isiokpo, the soldiers there said they had been taken to Umuahia. She gave them Bendic's full name, she described him, she told them he was her husband, that his parents were very old. Then she told them he was not a saboteur, that this was just the handiwork of enemies in the village. That day, people in Isiokpo began to pack and run away, since there was news that Nigerian soldiers were approaching and shelling villages as they went.

She rode back to Ogibah with Ireju, thinking of Bendic in a darkened cell, being tortured to give some information he didn't have. When she thought of the people she had heard being killed on suspicion of being saboteurs, her heart sank to her stomach, but she told herself that Bendic would not be taken from her permanently.

Two months later, the same wicked man who had reported Bendic to the authorities, this man whose name Ma refused to mention to her children, returned, as he claimed, from "headquarters" and reported that he had seen Bendic being executed. He claimed he had been standing right there when they put a rifle to Bendic's head and blew it away. Neighbors gathered around Ma's locked door as she screamed in her room and banged on the wall.

Bendic's mother didn't weep or blame anyone for her son's death—not the Ogibah man who made the false report, not the soldiers, nor the war. She spoke quietly of her own folly. Her regret was simple: She should have made the soldiers take her along when they came to arrest Bendic, or provoked them to shoot her and her son right there. Instead, what had she done? She had begged them like the wretched woman she was. She had sworn to them that her son had done nothing wrong; she had pleaded with them to sit down to eat, to put something in their stomachs for the long journey they had ahead. Hadn't they traveled far to get here? She told them she was Biafran, not Nigerian; she spoke the little Igbo she knew, but it did not do. They ate her food and carried her son away. Now that they had murdered him, was her suffering not far worse than death?

Four days later, when she did not get up in the morning, everyone knew she couldn't really have been expected to survive such a blow.

The war came to an end the following month, and Ma ambled about the house like a dark hen. A not so young widow with an old father-in-law and no children to speak of. Weeks passed, and then one day she got word from an old friend in Port Harcourt that detainees had been released and people were finding relatives they had thought were executed. The government had dumped them at the Municipal Primary School in Diobu, announcing over the radio for people to go claim their relatives. Ma made her way to Port Harcourt that same afternoon. She said her spirit told her that Bendic was among them. That he was alive.

"Nobody there looked like Ben," she told her children. As she had turned to leave the school grounds, covered with sick, dying men, she heard the whisper from a body lying on the ground next to her feet, a quiet voice saying her name. She looked at the shrunken body. The gaunt skull looked too heavy for his neck to carry. She looked in his eyes and knew it was him. She carried him on her lap, weeping all the way as the taxi took them home.

Eight years after the war, the children's grandfather passed away. He was aged eighty-one and died of natural causes, as they say. Something happened to Bendic right after, and he became a Christian. Their grandfather died in January, Ma got pregnant in February, Bendic got baptized in May, and Paul was born in November.

Ajie remembered this story one day and then sat in his room feeling sad for Bendic because he was an orphan. Ajie had always known his grandparents were dead, but it never occurred to him to think of it in those terms regarding Bendic. Things were going well between him and Bibi, so he confided in her.

"Don't be foolish," Bibi said, laughing, "grown-ups can't be orphans."

"Says who?"

"Says me."

"If Ma and Bendic have an accident now, God forbid, and die," she further explained, "we can become orphans. They'll probably take you to a motherless babies' home. Me and Paul to a remand home, I think. That's where they normally take the youths, because we are more difficult to handle."

Ajie looked away and scratched his chin.

They took the matter to Paul, who, after listening to Bibi's detailed explanation, took out a heavy *Oxford Advanced Learner's Dictionary* and read aloud to them. " 'Orphan,' " Paul began, " 'noun. A child whose parents are dead. Verb (be orphaned) (of a child); be made an orphan.' " Paul put away the dictionary. "And Bibi, stop wondering about the death of your parents. It can bring bad luck."

"I don't believe in bad luck," Bibi said, squinting, "and anyway, it wasn't me who started it."

Ajie had walked away. That night, in defiance of Bibi's correctness, he wrote in his notebook: "Bendic is an orphan. He was orphaned in 1978."

Baptized and renewed by immersion in the murky waters of Idu waterside. The white-robed choir lifted their voices on high, stamping their feet on the muddy bank; their harmonies carried across the swamps. It was a really big thing. Ma said they had spent the whole of the previous day cooking, making preparations to entertain guests. If people threw big parties when they bought secondhand cars, how much more for when they were being accepted into the Beloved, into heaven's gates?

Ma gave birth to a boy six months later, and they named

him Paul. By the time Bibi was born, Bendic had returned to his cool regard of religion, neither approving nor objecting, cherry-picking things he fancied in any faith. When Bibi asked him one day why he didn't pray before eating, as Ma made everyone else do, he said, "But I'm always praying, Bibi, especially when I'm asleep." Bendic's attitude had never stopped Ma from doing his before-food prayers for him. Whether they were eating from the same plate or if Bendic was eating alone, Ma would let her palm hover over the dish and shut her eyes, mumbling a quick "Thank you Lord for this meal. Bless, sanctify, and replenish the source." Bendic would say, "Amen," then wash his hands in the side bowl.

When the Jehovah's Witnesses knocked on their gate on weekends, Bendic allowed them to sit with him for an hour or more, much to Ma's disapproval. Ma said the Jehovah's Witness people twisted Scriptures. Did they not say Jesus Christ was only an angel and was not the Son of God or God incarnate, as true Christians believed? Bendic said he didn't see the harm in having a nice chat sometimes. There were times he refuted some of their doctrines and arguments because, as he told his children after the Jehovah's Witnesses were gone, "teachings like that can only have a negative effect on people. And people are what matter, not any religion or idea."

When the family traveled to Ogibah and the attendants from the Ntite shrine came around to greet Bendic in their long black skirts and eyes charged red from home-brewed gin, Bendic would answer loudly as they called him by his praise names. He would ask for them to be entertained. Ma said it was unnecessary to bring those kinds of people so close, "you can help them from afar." And Bendic replied, "Just because they believe in a different fairy tale from you doesn't make them evil."

"Benedict!" Ma made an angry face. "What I believe in is not a fairy tale."

Ma sometimes called him a fallen saint, a lapsed Christian, a backslider, but then she would counter herself almost immediately by saying to the children that their father was truly a Christian at heart and that was where it really mattered.

There were also times when she would jokingly tell him it was Ntite, the spirit of his family shrine, that was preventing him from being a serious Christian. "What is that other name they call Ntite? *He ajabe okwu.* If Ntite only resides in the dark, it's only natural that he would want to cast some of his shadows on the lighted path before you."

"Rubbish talk," Bendic would say.

"It's the truth."

Ajie liked it when they argued like this, when there was a tinge of irritation in Bendic's voice and a cruel ring of laughter in Ma's. Ajie had no interest in siding with losers, so he would set himself in the center of their argument, ready to join Bendic's camp if he was trumping Ma; if Ma began to show signs of victory, Ajie would defect to her camp. It did not really matter to him, at least not yet.

Their grandfather's name was Thomas Awari Utu. He took the name Thomas when he began his education in the Native Infant School at Omoku. But he was no infant at the time. This was 1911, and Awari was thirteen years of age. The story of how he began his education had become part of their family legend.

One day a slave in his father's household had persuaded Awari to join him at the new school that had opened at Ogbo

Onosi, on the eastern bank of Omoku River. Slaves were compelled to turn up at school to make up the attendance quota imposed by warrant chiefs. Freeborn, however, were allowed to do as they liked. The trek to Omoku would take roughly one hour if they traveled through the forest. Back then, Bendic informed the children, the British colonial government hadn't registered as firm a presence in Ali-Ogba as it had in other parts of the region. The swamps were too treacherous. So while Anglican and Catholic missions wrestled each other and schemed for converts, and tax collectors came down heavily on farmers in other parts of the region, Ali-Ogba was pretty much left alone and continued more or less undisturbed in its traditional ways. Now a native court had been set up in Omoku, and a school, which had the same premises as the new Anglican mission.

This was before they carved out the wide road that ran from Ahoada to Omoku; before various Christian missions set up shop and spread through the region with a zeal that put shrines to torch; long, long before the oil explorers appeared in their coveralls, hard hats, and jungle boots, tramping through the forests with government permits in their hands, muddying the clear water of the streams, scattering the fish, displeasing swimmers and fishermen alike. Pipelines did not crisscross the swamp. No huge gas flames flared.

So, here is Awari, thirteen years of age. Ajie imagines him in shorts only, no shirt, on this morning as they beat through the scrub and high forest. He and his slave, sidestepping the ponds and marshland and arriving, wide-eyed and with muddy feet, before the headmaster of the school, a man from Old Calabar named Ebok.

"You look like twins," Ebok says as he looks up from his books and levels his eyes on the boys. "Didymus," he pronounces, looking at Awari. "It's the Latin word for *double*. Your name will be Thomas. You know the apostle of Christ Thomas Didymus?"

That was how their grandfather Awari got himself a Christian name and eventually an education.

When Thomas Awari died, there was a dispute regarding where he should be buried. The Seventh Day Mission, the first church in Ogibah, a church he was instrumental in planting, decided the body of their patriarch belonged to them. The parcel of land that the church sat on was his. Everyone knew he was devout. He was an elder in the church and husband to one wife. He never swore to anything, nor once, since becoming a convert, joined in celebrating the New Yam Festival. The church said his body was rightfully theirs; he should be buried on the church grounds next to the schoolyard, the school he founded that bore his name. But the elders of their *onuobdo* had their own mind. They didn't pay attention to the churchmen. Their brother's body was theirs, naturally, and what they chose to do with it was entirely their own business. They would bury the man in the earth of his former bedroom.

Bendic made it clear to both parties that he intended to bury his father in peace and without much delay. They could choose to cooperate or forget about participating. A compromise was reached: Bendic's father was buried, after a traditional wake, in his bedroom, as was the custom for a man his age, but a Christian funeral service was held as well. Scriptures were read out loud into the clear morning air, hymns sung in their complete stanzas, but the family did the actual interment of the body. The casket was borne on the shoulders of the young men of their *onuobdo,* and the Seventh Day pastors trailed meekly behind in the funeral entourage.

From this single episode, Ajie decided, you could read the prognosis of their family's downfall. He would trace lines, join them in his moments of confusion, and arrive at solid conclusions. Their grandfather, who gave his entire adult life to the running of a church and school, could not, in his death, be fully claimed by them. He who rejected, in life, the old ways for the new; in death had his body prepared by men who sipped, gurgled, and spat twice at the shrine of Ntite. Draw yourself a straight line, walk backward on it to erase your footsteps, and you will trip and crack your skull. Straddle the two sides of a stream and you will unhinge your hips. Be unstable as water and you will not excel.

CHAPTER FIVE

S o here they all were, sitting at the dining table, feeling satisfied after eating Ma's delicious pancakes. It was Easter break, and as expected for that time of year, there was a light shower of rain outside. Bendic and Ma looked thoroughly pleased with themselves, and Ajie couldn't account for the reason why. They looked like they might just get up, link hands, and go for a stroll—if the rain abated—up and down the driveway, after which Bendic might grow thoughtful and unreachable, retreating into his study, or he might be inspired to take an afternoon nap in the bedroom, where Ma would join him and they would be private. Or Ma, being an occasional Bible reader, would search out her King James and make scriptural recommendations to Bendic and the children. She sometimes favored those poetic verses in the books of Proverbs and Ecclesiastes that extolled the virtues of a Good Woman: The virtuous woman commands her household after her in the way of the Lord. Early she rises and by night her lamp still burns, her hands never idle. It was the sort of afternoon when Ma might decide to engage herself in needlework, mending clothes for her family; in fact, she was about to send Bibi to fetch her sewing kit when Paul nearly blew up the house with his angry outburst.

How did his voice get so deep and big and no one noticed? He had only just turned eleven. Ajie was seven and Bibi was somewhere in between.

"I hate my school!" Paul roared. "I will die if I go back there."

And for no reason at all.

Bendic and Ma snapped back into the new reality unfolding before them. Ajie reclined in his chair, waiting for the action to begin. Bibi didn't seem moved. She'd had it up to here in the past few days with Paul's moodiness. Now he was just shamelessly seeking attention.

Any other parent—which was to say any normal parent—would have smacked Paul for such a display of ingratitude (do you not know that there are plenty of children who would give an arm in this country to get a good education?). Any other parent would have narrowed his eyes and issued a simple warning—"Let me not hear that nonsense again"—but Bendic just looked up at Paul and asked: "Why? Why do you hate your school?"

Ma didn't wait for Paul to respond. "If you are being bullied, I am going straight to your principal on Monday."

"I don't want to go to a day school," Paul began, but the Power Authority interrupted, the bulbs in the parlor lit up, and Bibi shrieked with joy, "NEPA!" She leaped to the TV and radio and turned both on at once, the volume drowning all of their concerns for a few seconds, until Ma snapped, "Turn them off!"

Paul's outburst was forgotten until the next morning.

The children are all dressed for school and having breakfast. Ma is looking at her watch; she has to drop Paul at his school before she heads to work. Bibi and Ajie will go with Bendic in his car, but right now Paul is in the bedroom, his meal untouched. "Paul, your food is getting cold. I don't want to be late, please. The traffic on Aba Road is something else these days."

Paul is in the bathroom. They hear the toilet flush. Twice.

"Paul, are you feeling sick? I thought I saw you go to the bathroom already this morning. I have red-and-yellow capsules to give you, if that is the case."

No response.

"Paul! Are you still in the bathroom? Are you giving birth or what? What is the meaning of this nonsense this morning? So you won't be happy until you make me late for school? I am conducting assembly this morning, and I have a staff meeting."

The toilet door opens. Paul comes out, face long like rope, makes his way into the parlor, passes them at the dining table, where his food sits abandoned, and enters the kitchen. Ma's impatient heels click-clack after Paul into the kitchen, but when she speaks, her voice is quiet and gentle. "What is the matter?"

"I told you the other day, that I'm tired of being a day goat."

"Day goat? What kind of talk is that? What's wrong with being a day student? Is it because your friend Fola is attending a boarding school? Let's talk about this after school. Please carry your bag and get in the car."

She packs Paul's breakfast and pours his tea into a thermos so he can eat on their way to school.

During the holidays, Ajie and Bibi learned that Paul would be attending a boarding school from the next term; he would begin class two.

In the weeks that followed, Ajie and Bibi choked in their collective longing. Paul's grades were excellent, so he would get a coveted place at a federal government college, where students were rarely admitted in second form. Their parents lit up like torches and burned with pride. There was nothing else they talked about that holiday. They took Paul for the four-hour drive to the school, even though it was closed and there was really nothing much they could see. Why hadn't they thought of this all along? They chided themselves. They should have registered Paul for the common entrance examinations, so he could get a place from form one. Surely Paul would have made it on the merit list to any federal school of his choice in the country. Then Ma cautioned that being very far away was not too good; this one was far enough. Bendic said boarding school helped children develop independence; it got them ready for the world. Ma said the academic standards of the federal schools were much higher than those of the expensive private schools.

Bibi had already found a book with the list of all federal colleges in the country and begun to deliberate about which schools to apply to. The farther away they were, the more desirable they became. "F.G.C. Sokoto is definitely where I'll be going," she said. "I don't like the idea of an all-girls school, or F.G.G.C. Potiskum would have been more like it." She asked Ma if she could use the phone, then spent over an hour talking to her friend Dawari, asking if she would also choose F.G.C. Azare so they could go together.

"Why up north?" Ma asked. "What happened to the one here in Port Harcourt, or Calabar?"

Bibi was having none of it; she pushed farther, to the desert borders of Chad and Niger Republic. "Do you think Bauchi will be cool?"

But the time for applying to schools hadn't come, so she just sailed about the house with a special brand of envy that translated into utter selflessness when it came to anything having to do with Paul's new school. "Ma, look at that bucket. Please buy it for Paul so if his dorm showers aren't working, he can have a bucket bath instead. Ma, please buy those rubber sandals for

Paul, the rainy season is coming, and you don't want him to destroy his leather ones in the rain. Ma, rain cape. Ma, you haven't marked Paul's things with his name. They will steal everything from him! You have no idea what goes on in dormitories."

Bibi became an expert in boarding school matters. Dawari's brother attended a school up north and supplied them with the most harrowing stories of his experience. The bullying by senior students, mattresses that disappeared from bunks after night prep, leaving the unfortunate victims no choice but to sleep on the bare springs. In an attempt to teach one junior boy a lesson he would never forget, a senior boy connected a wire from the live socket on the dorm wall and delivered shocks to the junior boys' genitals. Rather than discouraging Bibi and her friend, these stories terrified and excited them and made them want to go all the more. This was what they wanted: to be persecuted, to suffer some of these horrible things just so they could have the pleasure of telling the stories. Bibi helped Ma with stitching Paul's initials on the inside collar of his shirts. She told Ma that red oil paint was clearly the best to mark Paul's buckets and jerricans with, so he would be able to spot them from a mile away. Theft of buckets and jerricans was the order of the day at boarding schools. Bibi knew it all.

Paul was going to a new life. A life of padlocks and keys, cutlasses, sportswear, day wear, and six-spring mattresses. Ajie wished he were going in Paul's place. Ajie knew Bendic kept the school's prospectus in the top drawer of his desk, so when no one was about, he sneaked into the study and brought out the sheaf of beige A4 leaves held together by a spiral binding. He ran his fingers over the bold Baskerville font in which the school name was printed, then the coat of arms; he read aloud to himself the motto, which was in Latin, *Pro Unitate,* below that were address, phone numbers, reference number. Then the letter began: "Dear Parents/Guardians."

There were several lists: required books, provisions allowed in school, a list of contraband marked with asterisks, and then a footnote warning that the contraband list wasn't exhaustive. There were pages with drawings of the design of the school uniforms and day wear, and sample clips of the recommended fabrics.

As compensation, or maybe just his way of laying claim to Paul's future boarding school experience, Ajie set off with reading all the recommended books they had bought for Paul. The integrated science text had glossy picture pages that smelled fresh, like new money. He thumbed through diagrams of the human respiratory system, as well as the skeletal, digestive, and reproductive systems. There were fourteen textbooks in all, excluding the two novels that were required reading for English, and the Revised Standard Version of the Bible, which had a stiff cover.

One afternoon Bibi saw Ajie curled up on the couch reading Paul's copy of the novel *The Unknown Tomorrow.*

"You are not supposed to read that!" Bibi said, wounded.

Feeling guilty and surprised at being caught, Ajie quickly lowered the book and frowned.

"You are not old enough to read that book. Wait until I tell Paul. And by the way, who permitted you to touch it in the first place? Do you want to tear it?"

"I don't tear books," Ajie shot back defiantly.

"Shut up!" she yelled, and stormed out of the room.

⏳

Before Paul started attending boarding school, the children seldom stayed in their rooms during the day. They would return from school, slip out of their uniforms into house clothes, and then have lunch. Lunch was always *eba* and soup. It didn't occur to Ajie then that people could have anything else for lunch on a weekday. Ma served the *eba* for all three children in one plate. She would part the heap in the center to let off steam, which made it look like a volcanic eruption. She served the soup in three little bowls from which the children chose by order of seniority. There were times when Bibi wasn't sure which bowl to choose after Paul had taken his. She was certain there was a substantial difference in the quantity of soup or the size of meat in the two bowls, and she wasn't ready to pass up the benefits of her seniority to Ajie in any way, so she looked carefully. She would tilt the bowl to one side to allow a better look at the chunk of meat, which was otherwise partly submerged in the leafy soup. Ajie would watch her in a slow burn, wanting to run into her like a road accident.

One afternoon, without even having thought it, Ajie heard himself say, "Touch and take." Paul was waiting for them so he could start eating; his right hand was already out of the side basin, glistening with water.

"You should have said it before I started," Bibi said with vague determination. "You can't suddenly make a rule in the middle of something." Reading Ajie's interference as an indication, she picked the bowl she hadn't touched yet, certain it was the bigger portion.

"I think it's a good rule to adopt," Paul said.

"Stop taking sides," Bibi said.

"I'm not taking sides. I just said it's a good rule. Besides, it will apply to all of us," Paul said, "and why are you so fussy about choosing, anyway? There's hardly ever any difference."

Ajie liked it that the rule actually stood a chance. Only his timing was faulted. Touch and take would become standard practice. No one would question it ever again. Ajie smiled. They always tried to finish their *eba*. Ma didn't like to see leftovers in the bin, so they would make an effort to eat up all the *eba* and soup and then carry on leisurely with whatever chunks of meat came with the soup. The meat was always eaten last. If *eba* was the labor, then meat was the reward. Ajie would come to think of people who ate or touched their meat before finishing the rest of the food as badly brought up.

After lunch, the three of them would sit at the dining table to do their homework, then go outside to play within the compound. Ismaila would sometimes let them out to play at Fola's house.

When Paul returned from boarding school the first time, he started staying in the room to read. He would lie in bed all afternoon with a book held over his face and come out to the veranda to continue only when it was getting too dark in the room but was too early to turn on the light. He would carry on with his novels while eating, turning pages with his other hand. He also started reading newspapers. One day Bendic was in the parlor having a conversation with Mr. Ifenwa. Ma had gone to the salon to have her hair retouched, and after that, if there was time, she had said to Bendic, she would drop by the market on her way back.

It was a Saturday afternoon, which was to say the worst time on television. Breakfast TV and *Wrestlemania* ended at ten A.M., and so the rest of the day was a stint of boredom, all sorts of obscure field sports with rules that never made sense to any of the children no matter how hard they tried to follow. One dull game would follow the other until, finally, the mini-series *Things Fall Apart* came on at eight P.M.

When Mr. Ifenwa arrived, the children vacated the sitting area. They idled and thumbed through encyclopedias where they sat in the dining space, behind the room divider, the long back of the TV, the video player, the video rewinder, designed like a miniature piano, the wooden back of the big vinyl stereo, which was seldom played, and then all the plugs and sockets and a mesh of tangling wires. A tennis game was in play as Bendic talked with Mr. Ifenwa. There was the sound of the ball meeting the racquet and bouncing on the lawn court and a voice that kept going, "Fifteen love," "Thirty love . . ."

Paul went to the sitting area and took the weekend *Guardian* newspaper from the side stool, and as he walked back with it, Bendic said, "Paul, return that when you finish, I haven't read it yet."

"Oh." Paul hesitated for a moment, and Bendic said, "No no no, go on. Just return it once you finish."

Mr. Ifenwa, who was laughing through a story he had been telling, waved to Paul to go ahead, as if to say, *Don't mind me.*

Ajie thought perhaps this was what happened to you when you went to secondary school—something flicked in your brain that made you suddenly enjoy reading newspapers.

"Newspapers are boring, Paul," Bibi said.

"Sometimes there are important stories in them," Paul said.

"That's my point: They are only important stories."

"And important is boring?" Paul asked without looking up for her answer.

"Well," she said, twisting a lock of her hair plaits, "all the newspapers I've read are boring, and they were supposed to have important news in them."

"As if you've read any," Ajie said. He had never seen her read a newspaper.

"Look at you," she said, pointing at him, "you think I'm like you."

"Look at you. You think I'm like you," Ajie imitated.

"My friend, get out."

"My friend, get in."

"Shut up!"

"Shut down!"

She didn't get up to slap him, so he didn't reach out to slap her back.

On Monday, when Marcus came home to pick up Bendic's lunch, he handed Paul a copy of the day's *Guardian*. "Oga say make I give you."

Bibi looked around in mock wonder and laughed, taking the paper from Paul. Paul took it back from her and looked at Marcus as if expecting further instruction from Bendic on what to do with the paper. Marcus carried Bendic's lunch from the table, and as he drove off, Paul ran out to the veranda and shouted, "Tell him thank you."

That was how Ajie got used to seeing Paul read newspapers like a grown-up. Ajie didn't want to pretend or anything, so he stuck with reading storybooks. The following day, when Bibi joined Paul in the reading of daily newspapers, Ajie just sighed and went outside and started hitting the iron bars on the veranda with a piece of metal until Paul screamed, "Ajie!" and he wanted to scream back "Paul!" but instead kept quiet and went back inside.

Paul was lying on the sofa reading. Bibi was next to him

with a section of the paper he had passed on to her. A wind came through the open windows, billowing the curtains. The paper flapped about, and Bibi held it away from her face with one hand. She was reading the horoscope page. She had read out Ajie's horoscope for the week and now turned over to the next page, where the cartoons and the crossword puzzles were.

Ajie lay there on the couch, looking at his brother and sister. Ma's deep freezer hummed and whizzed in the kitchen like a fat man sleeping. Ajie looked up at the high ceiling of the parlor, at the cream voile curtains, at the dead gray face of the TV, and then at Bibi, who was biting the top of a pencil, frowning at the crossword. When Paul turned a page, the newspaper rustled like a cookie package and got out of shape. He beat it into place with the flat of his hand, straightened it out, and changed to a sitting position.

"There is a wall gecko above your head," Ajie said.

Paul looked up. The gecko was flat on the wall, head down. "They don't bite," he replied, and continued his reading. "Serves them right," he said sharply into the open face of the newspaper.

"What happened?" Ajie asked.

It was one of the usual stories they'd heard from their parents: A commissioner had been accused of embezzling government funds. Ajie didn't feel he had to read it to know what it was about. It was the same story every day, with different names and scenarios. But Paul read it with interest, and when he talked about it later, his normally expressionless face would take up shapes and form a picture of seriousness. He told Ajie that it was probably just the case that the disgraced commissioner had crossed someone higher up, and that was why he was being exposed. "It's not as if these people care about us," he said.

Now, this was what Ajie wanted, this way that Paul had of becoming something after he had read about it; this way he had of claiming things for himself. He had joined himself to a we, an us. A corrupt official had been exposed in the papers for misappropriating pension funds, and Paul was expressing betrayal, even anger, about it.

How do you make yourself do that? How do you learn how to work yourself up over something that's not directly your concern?

The stories in the newspaper sounded more interesting when Paul talked about them. Ajie never would have been interested in artificial fuel scarcity until Paul explained it to him and Bibi. Or Paul's bizarre theories about the bloody conflict between the Tiv and Junkun communities in the middle belt state of Benue. Ajie didn't care about those, either, but he listened. He enjoyed more than anything else the giddy warmth, the moral high of when Paul said "us," including him as part of the masses. This was something true and important, and it heated Ajie up.

"Don't worry about it," Paul said, stopping much too soon that day. He picked up an enormous Harold Robbins novel he had started reading; on the cover was a green-eyed brunette who had red luscious lips and a fur coat draped around her shoulders.

What is that book about? Ajie wanted to ask Paul, but on occasion even he felt reluctant about being a constant nuisance to people, and he could see Paul didn't want to be disturbed, so he went into the kitchen to get some ice cubes to chew. When he returned to the parlor, Bibi had put aside the newspaper and was reading a shoddily printed copy of *Efuru* that they had found while rummaging through Fola's garage and were now taking turns reading by order of seniority.

"When are you going to finish the book?" Ajie asked Bibi.

"Just about five pages left." Bibi thumbed through what was left of the book, "it's sooo interesting, should I tell you the story?"

"No."

"You can be so grumpy sometimes. Why?"

"I don't want to hear," Ajie said, and then threw the second ice cube into his mouth and began to crunch it.

Bibi couldn't hold herself back. "It's about this marvelous Oguta woman . . . oh, I really like her. She was very beautiful and loved by her husband, but she was barren, and her mother-in-law didn't want her."

"You are just looking for trouble," Paul said to Bibi.

"It's not as if I'm going to spoil it for him. It's so tragic," Bibi purred, and sank back into the sofa. "Okay, I'll just say this one thing and leave it there: I think someone dies at the end."

Ajie looked at her. He would refuse to read the book just to spite her. He would fling it back at her and tell her to return it, since he didn't want to read it anymore. He imagined she would feel something as sharp as pity mixed with guilt, and she would try to make it up to him somehow, but he wouldn't give her the chance.

"Do you know," Bibi was already saying to Paul, "that in France, crimes of passion are forgiven? I read something like that in one of Bendic's journals. There was a woman who killed her husband with a fork during an argument, and she wasn't jailed for murder."

"Temporary insanity," Paul said, "but it depends on the circumstance and on many other things."

"Port Harcourt is not Paris," Ajie quipped at Bibi.

"True."

"Nigeria is not France." Like he hadn't made his point.

Bibi threw him a glance and held his gaze for a moment, "Can't you just stop being annoying sometimes?"

Ajie yawned with his mouth wide open, covering it with his clenched hand.

Years later, each time he heard *crime of passion,* he would think of a woman in Paris with a fork in her hand, but more than that, he would think of the woman in a story Ma had told them. A story that sounded like it happened in the olden days but which Ma said only took place after the war. She said she knew the family, and that after the tragic event, a ballad was composed that spread through all of Ogba land and didn't go out of season for many many years.

There was this woman from Erema who would leave her husband and move in with a man whose house was on the farther side of the same village. As was the custom, leaving your husband in that way was an accepted (if reproachable) way for a woman to initiate divorce. After that an amicable settlement could be reached, and the legal aspects of ending the marriage would be embarked on. This involved returning the bride-price paid by the husband's family.

This woman would leave her husband and stay with the second man for many days, sometimes a whole year, and each time her husband would go to her people to plead with her to return to him. Her people would put pressure on her and she would return to her husband, but soon after, the affair would resume. Her husband sent emissaries to beg the man to leave his wife alone, but nothing changed. One day the husband took a machete and chopped off the head of his wife's lover. Then he carried the head and walked the whole length of the village, and each time he met someone, he asked, "This thing I have done, is it good or is it bad?," and the person would answer, "It is right what you have done, it is good." And when he reached the end of the village, he killed himself: exactly what was expected of a man who had taken the life of another.

The children named her "the love woman," even though Ma never mentioned the word *love*. Ma always rendered the account in a few sentences, just as it had happened. She seemed to be in awe of the story each time she told it, as if saying to her children, "This is something that has happened in the world. This is what can happen in the world." It was Bendic who called it a "costly affair." It was Bendic who once said with a sigh, "Desire is blind." It was also Bendic who wondered aloud about which was the worse punishment for their affair, "to be the one beheaded or be the one who survived to live through the aftermath?"

But whatever there was to know about desire and its costs was beyond Ajie then. He was at that time completely passionate and pure. He imagined himself, his brother, and his sister to be people who would shoot into the world and burn, fiery arrows set free by their parents from their home here at number 11. They would love greatly and do useful things. Bibi would become rich and important and build houses and hospitals for the poor. Paul would simply change the world.

But what would that cost?

As for desire, Ajie knew well about animals mating, he had read about and fairly well understood the mechanics of human sex, but this was before that holiday when Ma and Bendic had to go to America for two weeks and sent them to spend the time with their uncle Tam, who lived in D-Line. It was in that D-Line house that he had his first intimations of desire. It was in that house, in an upstairs room with netted windows that gave onto a moss-covered fence where an Agama lizard watched and nodded, that he, Ajie, lay beside Barisua, Uncle Tam's house help, who was breathing softly after he had touched her and she had touched him back.

II

The blue Peugeot 504 station wagon moved slowly down the narrow road. A woman on a bicycle coming from the opposite direction paused to make way, one foot on the ground. She leaned into the bush and peered into the passing vehicle. There was hesitation, then the quick light of recognition catching on her face. She waved, shepherding her bicycle out of the bush as the car passed.

"Slow down," Bendic said to Marcus as they approached the bend. Stalks of grass slapped against the car window. Damp leaves clutched and slid past like hands. Two children ran onto the road, rolling an old car tire. They sighted the station wagon and stood for a while in their underpants to watch it pass.

"They should have done bush cutting by now," Ma said, looking out the window to the high thicket on the roadside. "OYF is not serious anymore." By which she meant the Ogibah Youth Front, whose obligations included road clearing and other maintenance work around the village, especially during preparations for the festive seasons.

The two children by the road waved, then ran back the way they'd come. Ajie's eyes followed them as they ran rolling their tires, but the narrow path and clustering trees made it hard to see the house they disappeared into at the end of the path: a mud house, he imagined, built of mud, wattle, and wood beams, plastered and smoothed with clay; there would be an open veranda with a bench on it, an airy front room with benches and stools where the man of the house would remand a reclining chair for himself; a kitchen by the side constantly exhaling wood smoke. And beyond all that, at the far reach in the back, an orchard of orange trees, tangerines, sour sop, ube and kola trees, a pit latrine with a neat clearing around it.

They drove past the cemetery where Christians were buried. No headstones, just knee-high grass. Nwokwe's house was one of the few that stood clearly visible from the road. A visitor to town would be mistaken to count these houses and then decide on that basis there weren't many people about. At a moment's notice, a band of able-bodied youth could appear from nowhere: to answer a distress call, to question a suspicious stranger, or to welcome someone long forgotten who had returned home. Stooping beneath and behind this moist August greenery, on both sides of the road, were century-old homesteads, each a thatched fiefdom within its rights, laden with legends of its own survival.

"Ogbuku has reroofed." Ma's eyes followed a flash from the new roofing, reflecting in the sun. Paul was sitting in front with the driver and rested his head on the window. Ajie knew he wasn't sleeping. Bibi sat in the back with Ajie, her eyes scanning the space from the front to the middle row, where their parents sat. "It's beautiful," Ma said of the stylish maroon-colored corrugated roofing.

"I think it's hideous," Bendic said.

"I like that kind of red, it's not screaming," Ma replied.

"It doesn't go with the green paint of the house. It's a bit much," Bendic said, winding down his window. "I guess he's stealing enough money these days to have his walls gold-plated.

What is stopping him? I suppose it's not surprising that his father, Nwokwe, gives him no counsel."

"I saw Egoyibo the other day at the school board," Ma said. "She told me if you see the money that young man is spending building hotels in Omoku . . . obviously, it's not all his money. Why can't the Youth Front vote him out as secretary?"

"OYF is not what it was when it started. He has blocked their mouths with money. I hear he plans to run for local government councillor."

The car veered off the road, and their house was immediately in view—tall, white, alone, and at a distance. They went past the Seventh Day Mission. The churchyard was swept clean. A fruit tree stood to the side with an old car wheel slung on a low branch; an orderly struck it at appointed times to notify members of church activities.

Children suddenly appeared from everywhere, shouting, running toward the car, throwing themselves about. Marcus tooted the horn and the excitement thickened. The smell of carbide was in the air when Ajie stepped out. The four-day festival would commence in two days.

A cannon sounded from another quarter of the village to signal the countdown. The shrieking children scurried around Bendic and Ma, shouting greetings, jumping up and down, as they were rubbed on the head and asked about their parents. It was bedlam around the car while Bibi and Paul's friends gathered to talk to them, and Ma had to raise her voice to ask Paul to get her handbag from the car. "The house keys are in my bag."

Marcus opened the trunk, and some of Paul's friends moved closer to help with the luggage. Bendic was exchanging pleasantries with some of the older people who had just dropped by.

He moved closer to the trunk to oversee the off-loading, point-ing at items that should be left on the ground beside the car, nodding for some to be taken upstairs.

"Look how they have grown!" Ine exclaimed, slapping her-self across the breasts as she gaped at Paul, Bibi, and Ajie. She popped her eyes at the children, then back at Bendic as if the rapid growth had all been his doing. "Come come come." She beckoned and threw her arms open for the three of them.

"*Madi,*" Paul greeted first.

"*Mmayi,*" Ine responded.

"*Iye,*" Paul replied.

"*Ogbowu.*"

"*Iye,*" Paul replied again, completing the greeting, and then made his way back to the car.

Bibi was next in line. There were no shortcuts. Morning, noon, or night, the performance was always followed through.

"Your children speak Ogba like they never left this village for one day," Ine said to Bendic, looking impressed. Bendic shrugged as if to say it was the least expected of him.

Paul hurried past with another boy; they were holding a sack of beans between them.

"Careful," Bendic said, turning aside from Ine, "mind your backs."

Some other grown-ups came over to join Bendic and Ine. Ajie picked up his bag just as another man arrived and shook Bendic's hand.

"Your wife did not come with you?" Eleza asked Bendic.

"She has just gone inside," Bendic replied, pointing to the house, "to make sure these things are put in their right place." As if purely for the woman's pleasure, he added, "Does a car travel without its engine?"

"It does not happen!" the woman yelped with a clap of her hands, dizzying herself with laughter. More people arrived, saying greetings, repeating questions already answered. Ajie carried his bag upstairs and came back to find Ogunwa saying to Bendic, "It's good that you bring your children always."

"At least twice every year," Bendic said. "All their long vacations are spent here, and Christmas. Sometimes we are even here for the Easter break."

"You know, Josiah's children came home last year and couldn't even greet properly," Ogunwa said, then shook his head. "They were barking at their poor grandmother in English, saying they hated the village, they wanted to go back to Port Harcourt."

"You don't mean it."

"The question you should ask me is where was Josiah when all this was happening," Ogunwa said, looking Bendic in the face, ready to deliver his punch line. "He was in Port Harcourt! Dumped his children here and ran back with his driver the same day!"

There was a scattering of laughter.

Ajie walked past and wondered why people found silly stories like that amusing. He thought Bendic should be paying more attention to the off-loading. With all the trouble they went through in Port Harcourt, buying things over the week, packing and labeling gifts for different relatives, it would be a real shame to get things mixed up. Nne Nta's quarter bag of rice was being hauled past Ajie, the name tag taped to the sack flapping, almost falling off. The two gallons of kerosene had been set aside beside the car, but where were the bags of spices for the women in Ma's meeting?

Ma's voice cut through the din. Ajie saw one of his parents' friends setting his shiny stainless-steel White Horse bicycle securely on its stand. A package wrapped in a black bag was tied on the back carriage. "Application Master!" Ma called out, her own voice exciting her. "Application Master!" Each time he confirmed with "*Mmu-yagbe*. That is me." His face cracked open, and his tongue trembled as he laughed. He was dressed in tobacco-brown trousers and a shirt with the sleeves rolled up to the elbows. The red of the shirt had bled out until the color was now a dull brown. He put his hands up and called Bendic several times by his praise name. Bendic gave him a firm handshake and called him by his real name, Mark. Mark turned toward Ma and embraced her.

Mark and Ma had gone to the same primary school in Obite. The story went that after his standard six—this was back in the days when, according to Ma, a standard-six certificate was a rare thing and far superior to the university degrees awarded these days—Mark took his certificate and headed off to Port Harcourt in search of work. He spoke and wrote impeccable English; he could draft minutes, compose persuasive letters, and had a natural aptitude for quick learning. He applied for secretarial positions, clerk positions, office boy positions, but nothing was forthcoming. With his application letters and standard-six certificate in hand, he rose early every morning and went from office to office, through all of the old Port Harcourt town area and the new layouts, yet no job was offered to him. Meanwhile, in the village, his mother bragged about how her son had gone to get a white-collar job, how he had an excellent certificate; she said that son of hers was not at all made for farm work. When Mark returned to the village many months after, without a job or the promise of one, his mother, bewildered, asked him, "So what have you been doing?"

"I have been applying," he said to his mother. To show he hadn't been playing about in Port Harcourt instead of looking for a job, he went to his box and brought out a creased manila envelope that had gone soft, like cloth. Out of it he brought his application letters and his standard-six certificate, which was so worn that it was barely holding up in the middle where he had folded it. His mother took a look at it and said, "Well done." She was swamped at that moment by a sense of overwhelming dignity at her son's effort. He had been working so hard at making applications that he had ripped his certificate in half. As she later said to the other women, her son was the application master.

Even this afternoon, three pens were clipped on the breast pocket of Application Master's shirt: red, black, and blue, like an auxiliary nurse. There was an austere shine to the aging leather of his sandals.

Paul tapped his brother on the shoulder. "Make yourself useful," he said, "carry something else. See the yams." He gestured toward the car, and Ajie sauntered back, mumbling that Paul should let him be.

Ajie's friend Ossai arrived, and soon after Gospel and Uba joined them, and the whole posse buzzed their way upstairs.

"There is a spot at Uhwo where a buffalo is calving," Uba said.

"Liar! Everyone knows there are no buffaloes anymore in Uhwo."

"I swear, I can take you this evening, or tomorrow morning if you are free."

"A grass cutter got caught in my trap," Ossai said, "at Uhwo, too." Soon the trap would claim a deer, he boasted. When should they go see his lucky spot? But the dances were beginning, they needed to go cut raffia to get the skirts for the outfits.

"Tomorrow, if the weather holds."

"Whether the weather holds or not," Uba insisted, "we have to cut the raffia, latest tomorrow. It's important." Their voices and the noise of their footsteps bounced about, echoing as if the staircase were an empty house.

Bendic sat on the puffed armchair in his parlor. His chest hair was a mesh of gray, and the low mound of his belly heaved gently. Ma's sequined blouse was up on a hanger on the balcony, airing in the breeze. She had changed into a laid-back flowered round-necked blouse that didn't matter.

Bibi burst into the boys' room. "Oh my God! I knew I would forget something! Paul, please check if I put my slippers in your bag by mistake."

"Very unlikely," said Paul.

"It's okay if you don't want to help," Bibi said, and turned toward Ajie. Paul unzipped his bag, rummaged through the sides, and asked her to have a look.

"What about you, Ajie?" Bibi asked, looking at his bag. Ajie pushed his unpacked bag toward her; she looked down at it for a second, then pulled out some clothes from the bag, felt inside hurriedly, and decided she may have actually left the slippers at home in Port Harcourt. She turned and walked out of the room without saying a word. They overheard her lament to Ma, who said something back to her in a low voice.

"Akabuka Market?" Bibi wailed. "I can't even believe you are suggesting that. Do you really think I will find that type of slippers in Akabuka Market, Ma?"

The sun began to cool and visitors trickled in. Some dropped in for a quick greeting, others sat down long enough to be offered something: kola nut and pepper, garden eggs, soft drinks, groundnuts. Paul and Ajie looked over the quadrangle from their window, watching the comings and goings.

Downstairs, a woman walked toward the door with her son in tow. He was head and shoulders taller but followed like he lacked all volition. Ajie felt this visit would have something to do with school fees, a school levy, or money to register for some final exam.

"Holding court," Paul said as he lifted the gauzy blind, then let it fall back to place.

"Kings hold court," Ajie said.

"Local magistrates do, too," Paul responded, not exactly sidestepping the combat his brother was trying to initiate. "I think Bendic should take up a chieftaincy. *Chief* before his name will suit him. I think he already performs the duties one way or the other. But you know Bendic."

"Chief Benedict Utu," Ajie enunciated slowly, lending the title its required weight. "It sounds good."

A shrill, angry falsetto rose from the parlor and stayed up. Raised voices weren't unusual during sessions at Bendic's parlor. Other voices joined in. Ajie could tell most of the men by their voices.

"Jonah," Paul said with a small laugh. "I wonder who he's giving the sermon to today."

"Don't worry, Ikpo will soon shout him down."

"Shout Jonah down? Are you kidding?"

Ajie always found Jonah amusing. Not just for his slight voice (and how it didn't match the deep lines on his face and the stoop of his shoulders) or how easily rattled he was, but the name, too. Weren't his parents aware of the fate of that Jonah in the Bible? The whole shipwreck business and living in the belly of a whale for three days? Ajie had read the story on many occasions and each time greatly relished Jonah's tantrums and self-pity, even though he thought him mean-spirited.

A man knocked on the door downstairs. He stood waiting, didn't try the door handle. Paul stuck his head out the window, greeted the man, and told him the door was unlocked, that he should just give it a push. The man made to push the door as Paul ran downstairs anyway to let him in, and Ajie followed.

The man had no upper lip. Half his face was gone, deep holes burrowed in by a childhood affliction of smallpox. Still, he wasn't hideous. He was tall and athletic, yellow like the sun. He was the high priest of the Ntite shrine. His name was Aduche, and they knew he had a great love for Bendic. Everything he had seen and knew of the world could be sensed in the quiet power of his gait as he stepped into the entryway. He placed his hand on Paul's cheek as he responded to their greeting. Ajie could smell the tobacco and wood smoke and something else on his clothes, and when he smiled at them, it was all gum. He looked down at Ajie for a brief moment. His gaze had a quality possessed by no one else Ajie had met in the whole world. It was something of a shared secret. It made him feel special; it seemed to be saying that he, Ajie, was useful in a way that was particularly important and that a time would come when this purpose would be made clear.

"Where is your father?" Aduche asked, as if he didn't know the way.

A hush had fallen over the crowd in the parlor, except for Bendic's voice, which kept rising and falling, strong, though the words were muffled to anyone standing in the stairway. Conscious of Aduche walking behind them, Ajie tried to keep pace with Paul, who was taking it slow, not skipping the steps two at a time, as he normally would. It was a stately procession, two boys marching to the altar with a high priest on their trail. It was Abraham with a dagger hidden by the girdle of his loin-cloth and Isaac in front of him, wondering where the sacrificial lamb was. Ajie knew if anyone had to pick between him and his brother that Paul would be preferred, Paul would be set aside for saving. But Abraham had to choose "the son whom he loved" to offer as a sacrifice. Why was he put to that kind of decision? Why and how was it possible for him to love one son more than the other? What was so terrible about Ishmael that his own father's love for him fell short, therefore disqualifying him as the worthy sacrifice? Why was Ishmael not preferred? Would Bendic love Paul enough to kill him if it were God Almighty asking him to give his most precious son?

These were questions Ajie needed answers to. But more, he wanted to be worthy. He wanted to be the son too difficult to give up, the one so greatly loved and therefore singularly suitable for sacrifice. Matters of this nature meant a huge deal to him between the ages of eight and nine. He would lie in bed at night and toss the questions around in his mind, and at some point, just so he could give himself some kind of answer to be able to go to sleep, he would decide what Bendic would do if he were in Abraham's shoes. But there was so much to consider before that. Where would Ma be when all this was happening? It was difficult to imagine her sitting quietly in the kitchen while Bendic wrestled with this dilemma.

This was what would happen. After listening to the Lord's command, Bendic would reply to the Lord Almighty, Maker of every living thing—the beasts of the fields, the birds of the air, and all the creatures of the sea, everything that walks, crawls, flies, and swims—"Leave my boys alone." That was exactly what he would say: "Leave my boys alone. If you want someone dead, by all means, here I am, and please do the killing yourself, don't make someone else do the dirty job." At which point Mr. Ifenwa would spring up and cheer from the crowd of witnesses, whistling at Bendic's courage, his thumb raised high, and then shouting: "Or just make him a prisoner of conscience!"

Paul pushed the screen door open and walked into the parlor, holding the door as Ajie followed him in. Bendic looked up at them; there was a pause in his speech as he held their gaze, was there a message for him, did they want something, or had they come to sit and listen? He finished his sentence as Aduche stepped into the parlor.

"Swoooooooy!" Bendic roared. "Swoy! *Agbra Obigor.*" Spirit of the bushes. Lord of Obigor forest. Bendic stood erect like a soldier in a parade as he called the high priest by his many praise names, then he doubled over, waist down, and greeted. Bendic gave Aduche twofold respect because he was from Bendic's mother's people. He *owned* Bendic.

"Should I rise?" Bendic kept asking after the greeting was over.

"Please," Aduche responded, "please rise, son of my sister."

"You are sure?" Bendic insisted as some laughter came from the crowd. The air in the room had lightened. Bendic straightened up, submitted to a hug from Aduche, and waited for the man to take a seat that had been vacated for him. "You arrived just in time. I was finishing." Bendic beckoned to Paul, and when he came close, he whispered in his ear, "Tell your mother to bring the whiskey. She should also put an unopened bottle in a bag for when Aduche is leaving."

Some of the faces in the room that day were not regulars in the house; some weren't particularly close friends of Bendic, although with the way things were in Ogibah, if someone wasn't your friend, it was very likely he was your brother. The lightness in the room did not last for long. There was something extra in the air that day. As Paul and Ajie went off to get the drink, they heard someone bang his fist on the table, and soon there was shuffling as two men were restrained from getting into a fight. Paul and Ajie hurried back with the whiskey in time to hear Nwokwe shouting.

"Let your father eat shit!" He pointed at Jonah, his red *kepe* nearly falling off his head. "You say I ate bribe from Company?"

Jonah advanced toward Nwokwe, shouting back, "Did I say it behind your back?"

"You say I ate bribe, can you swear? Do you have witnesses? Swear by Ntite, let's see whether you will last three days." Nwokwe snapped his fingers.

Some people pulled him away, asked him to be calm, to have some respect for the gathering and for Bendic, who had arrived from Port Harcourt only today, and for the elders here.

"Were you people not here when he accused me?" Nwokwe retorted. "You all saw him open his mouth to talk like someone born yesterday."

"I say you took money from Company," Jonah shot back. "You are exactly like your father, bowing down to paper money and coins. And as for that son of yours, ha!"

"There is no need for hot blood yet." Bendic raised his voice from where he sat in his armchair. The chair had wooden legs that ended in an imitation of the paws of a great bush cat. Bendic had been taking in the scene calmly, and now that he raised his voice, a little quiet returned to the room again, and eyes turned toward him. "It's a serious accusation Jonah is making." Jonah squeezed his face and nodded from where he sat on a bench. "Nwokwe is here with us," Bendic continued, "and can answer for himself, here in our presence. We will discuss what we can today and come back tomorrow if need be." Nwokwe's face was like an open sack of nails. "Let us all bear in mind," Bendic's voice soared in the still air of the room, "that this thing trying to rip us apart is actually coming from outside. If we don't understand that first, then we will be wasting strength on the wrong matter."

Heads nodded. "It's true," said one of the young men leaning against the wall. Seats had been arranged behind the sofa but weren't enough.

Application Master got up and called out greetings. He called out a few times before quiet fell on the place. An old man by the corner was shrugging, and his "Let them shut up so we can get to the bottom of this" was the only sound breaking the silence.

Application Master began to speak. "Our people say rather than let the antelope escape completely, let us at least slice off his tail." Grunts of approval from the crowd followed. It's true. It's true. "This meeting will continue tomorrow, but we are here already, so we might as well talk . . .

"Company has been here for nearly three decades. There are young men in this room who were not yet born when they came to tap oil from our ground. Nobody here can say we have treated Company badly. And that's not to say our stomachs are too sweet with happiness. What your God has blessed you with, you can't quarrel with it. You use it and move ahead in life, for your own good, for your children, and for your neighbor, too. Is it not so?" Application Master paused.

"It is so, it is so." More grunts from the crowd.

"Before Company came, we were here, the oil was here, right here." Application Master stamped his foot on the tiled floor. "Right here, under our feet. Did we make trouble when they came here combing through our forests? When they said the government sent them, did we not make way for them and even show them around? Did we not agree when they pointed at the places they wanted to dig their burrow pits and set their derricks? When their work destroyed our farms, when they cut through people's houses to build their pipelines, did we fight them or seize their workers so that their work would not go on? Did we not accept the money they paid for damages?

"Everyone here knows what happened in '71." A groan escaped some older people in the room. Someone echoed the year and snapped his fingers. "If you were too small," Application Master continued, "or not born yet, ask your parents, let them tell you what our eyes saw here in 1971. We have managed since then with Company—not friends, not enemies.

"Now that they have decided they want to build pipe for gas, not oil, they want the pipes to go through our farms and our waterside near Idu. I have only one question to ask: If the ones they built for oil are killing us now, why should we allow them to put up new pipelines when we don't know what damage they might cause?"

Nwokwe rose to his feet and his snuffbox clattered onto the floor, destroying the calm Application Master's speech had created. "If not for Company!" he shouted. He didn't even look down at the fallen item. Someone next to him picked it up to hand back to him, but he waved the hand away. "If not for Company, you think we would have been anything that we are today?" His voice was loud, like someone in the middle of a quarrel.

"This secondary school we have now, that our children attend—people from other villages come here now for school—how long did we stay before it was built? The only primary school we have, is there anyone in this room who doesn't know how that came about?" Nwokwe paused for a while, as if expecting someone to respond to his questions. "Did the government know us before now?" he asked, looking around the room. "Did any tarred road run to us before? Does this village lead to anywhere? So why do we talk as if we don't know these things? And because I speak my own truth, the truth that I see with my two eyes, does that mean I've accepted a bribe from outsiders against my own people?

"If not for Company, would we have the mono pump that gives us water? How many villages—count it yourselves—around here have tap water? Do they not drink from their wells still? Without Company, mosquitoes would be eating us up here in the mangrove, and all these people in the government wouldn't have known we even exist."

"So, you have not accepted money from anyone?" Bendic asked.

"He has eaten money, that is why his mouth is so sweet for them," someone said from the benches before Nwokwe could respond. Ajie saw it was Morgan, a muscular man who had a reputation as a radical member of the OYF.

"I want all of you to listen to what I am saying today and mark it on a wall somewhere," Nwokwe continued gravely. "Some of you forget we are a small people. All these bigger groups in this country who go in and out of government, do you think they would look in our direction if we didn't have oil? We can all disappear from here in a single afternoon, all of us in the whole twenty-four Ogba villages, and they wouldn't even notice. They wrestle for power among themselves as if we don't count. As our people say, when the elephants have a wrestle, it's the grass below that feels the stampede. One day you will say that I said it. All I want to tell you is this: Let us stay close to Company; what they are offering may not be the best, but we can't be claiming our rights and then lose out completely."

"They have offered you money," Ikpo said as he stood up, pointing a finger at Nwokwe. Ikpo was a man of about fifty. "They have offered you money, and you may have accepted, so that their gas pipes can run past behind your house. You think we are fools?" Ikpo's voice was level but hard. He looked like the sort of man who, in his younger days, would have invited whatever was to happen tomorrow to happen right now. "I won't blame you if you want to accept, or if you have accepted, but at least have the decency to keep your mouth straight when you speak. And as you are taking this money, do us a favor and tell them that pipeline shall begin and end at your house. It will be a very short pipeline. I don't know if anyone else here has grown soft enough in the head to join you. And if gas fire burns, it is your family who will be consumed, since you have decided to go deaf in both ears."

"So that is what you wish for me." Nwokwe's voice came back wounded. "That my family be destroyed. All of you sit down here and listen to what this man wishes on his brother."

"You will be the one wishing it on yourself," Ikpo retorted.

The meeting stretched until Paul and Ajie got bored and went downstairs to meet the other children at the usual place by the water tank stand, over which the house had thrown a huge shade. They sat on the rungs of the steel ladders, dangling their feet, catching up on things. The sun dipped toward Uhwo and turned the sky orange red.

CHAPTER SEVEN

A jie and Ossai emerged from the hedges and followed the path beside the flower fence. Someone watching
from the church would see only one head bobbing above
the flat top of the flowers. Ossai was a clear head taller, even
though he was barely two months older than Ajie.

They walked past the church and smelled the tannin that
was poured regularly all over the window and door frames
to keep termites away. Across the road, in the schoolyard, the
old gmelina trees stretched their vast branches and littered the
ground with fruits. Ossai stepped over them, but Ajie squashed
some underfoot, making the juice squirt, mapping their trail
with a darker, inky brown.

It was around seven-thirty in the morning, and they were
heading for a quick wash in a nearby swamp. Ajie had been
idling in bed when Ossai arrived; he told Paul he was going out.
He threw a bar of soap, a sponge, and a fresh change of clothes
into a plastic bag and left with his friend. Paul, who'd had an
early shower in the bathroom downstairs, was back in bed and
didn't look away from his book when Ajie spoke. Ajie and Ossai
shut the door to the staircase, and the house sank deeper into
that quietness houses often settle into right after breakfast at
holiday times, just before the steady flow of visitors begins.

"Gmelina stains never wash out," Ossai said as he looked

back at Ajie. His own fresh clothes were in a black cellophane bag clutched under his arm.

"I'm not wearing white," Ajie replied, "so it doesn't matter."

The edges of the school's football field were well marked, and at either end of the field was a standard-size goalpost. They walked past the classroom block to their right and then the school farm behind it, and by the corner was a path that led to the bush. Grass brushed against Ajie's ankles. He walked a few paces ahead of Ossai as they filed into the bush, taking care not to slip on the clay earth. Creepers, bracken, and bamboo emerged in a rush of darkish green, and the canopy of clustered trees dimmed the sun.

It felt odd to have appeared here, three minutes away from the road. And it wasn't just the filtered gloom and coolness. Each time he stepped into this swamp, Ajie felt that it claimed him, glazed and held him apart from the world outside.

They heard a rustle. Ahead of them was a man in a brown loincloth, climbing down a palm tree. He held on to a harness with one hand, and with the other he held a blue keg foaming with palm wine freshly tapped from the tree. They greeted him when they got to the foot of the palm wine tree, and he grunted back at them and continued his business.

The two boys came into a clearing where wild jewel orchids were pushing out their last flowers. They stripped and bunched their clothes together on top of a shrub by the pond. Ossai first gave his shorts a quick wash, rubbing and kneading the cloth as it squished out lather, then a final rinse. Ajie sat at the edge of the pond, dipped his toe in it, and flicked the water. He cleared the water lilies to a corner and squatted beside the pond, looking into the opaque green water. A warm crack of sunlight fell through the trees and touched his back. He dived. The splash was as loud as his dive was clumsy, and then a hush fell over the space. The water bubbled and rippled. It was as if the swamp held its breath for a few seconds and then let go in a rowdy babble that rose sharply among the startled birds in the trees.

"It's dangerous to dive in like that," Ossai said, easing into the water. "There are usually sticks at that end of the pond. People set their nets there sometimes, so you need to check first."

Ossai rubbed his head and body with a green soap that smelled clean and rubbery, like an eraser. Ajie climbed out of the pond and searched in his bag on the side. The green Palmolive soap was too big to hold in one hand, so he held it with both. He smeared it on his head and all over his body, then let himself back into the pond.

They dried themselves, and Ossai moved his drying clothes to a spot where the sun had gained ground. He shivered a little in the sunlight, then picked up a stone and flung it across the pond. It startled a little bird by the bank.

"Do you know the name?" Ajie asked as they watched the bird fly away.

"*Kpamboy,*" Ossai replied.

Ajie thought it might be a gray hornbill. "I wonder what it's called in English . . . not too sure," he said under his breath. The gray hornbill had yellow feet, but this one's feet were black. Ma's *Encyclopaedia of Tropical Birds* covered a wide range of species and had colored pictures. Ajie and Paul used to play Spot and Name and often had unresolved arguments over shades of plumage, length of tail, and birdcall. Ma, who was expected to have the last say in these matters, said that some of the species they found in Ogibah may not have been named in English. This response was unsatisfactory in the competitive atmosphere. "The rain forest," Ma would continue importantly, "supports the highest diversity of all living organisms the world over." She would transform into the schoolmistress before her classroom, a biology teacher dressed in calf-length georgette skirt and chiffon blouse, with a chalk in one hand and an efficient duster in the other.

Ahead, on top of a rotting palm trunk, a squirrel in its perfect camouflage coat stretched out, calm, disregarding. Ajie picked up a stone and aimed.

"The head is mine if you hit."

"I'll have to knock it dead first."

"The head is mine if you hit, like I said." Ossai waited for the shot. "And you'll need a bigger stone if you intend to harm it at all."

A siren went off that startled both Ajie and the squirrel. "Oh no!" Ajie shouted.

"It's ten o'clock," Ossai said.

"Where is it coming from?" Ajie asked.

Ossai felt the clothes to see if they were dry. The khaki shorts had a starched stiffness to them. He folded the washed clothes into the cellophane bag, hopped into the fresh shorts he'd brought along, put his shirt on, and left the button undone. "Base Camp," he replied.

"When did they start blowing this siren? I don't think I heard it when we came last year."

"Not sure when it started, but it's every Tuesday morning now, by ten. My father said it's a signal for the engineers to rest their drilling machines."

"Really?" Ajie said. "I'll ask Bendic when we get home."

"He will know better," Ossai said. "My father is just a night watchman at the Location."

"That doesn't mean he can't know why," Ajie said softly. "I just want to hear what Bendic will say."

They came out of the bush, and the sun bore down on them as they walked toward the school. The sun had baked everything it could reach, and the ground ahead of them shifted like steaming fluid.

"I'm sure by now they'll be looking for you."

"They won't. It's our holiday, and I can go anywhere I want," Ajie said. He wasn't some soft city boy who couldn't be away for a minute without being missed.

"Okay, then. Will you follow me to my house so I can check something for my mother?"

"Okay."

"I'll come back with you to your house."

"Okay."

Loud voices were already coming from Bendic's parlor as Ajie and Ossai came up the stairs. Ajie knew the parlor would be packed full of people. Bicycles were parked beside the door downstairs, and they both went upstairs and Ajie opened the door a bit, put his face through the screen door and scanned the crowd of men sitting.

Paul was with the young men who stood at the back. His bright blue T-shirt stood out among the tired old ones the others wore. Still, standing there with his face set and attentive, he was very much part of the group. When Ajie asked Paul later that evening what the meeting was about, Paul explained. "Company wants to give Ogibah one million naira for the new yam festival celebration." Ajie was in bed listening to Paul, who was in his own bed across the room.

"They want to build gas pipelines, too, and some people's farms and houses would be affected. They want to pay compensation. Mark thinks they should be made to wait. That if they give them an easy way, they would take us for granted, like they did in the past. He said, 'Why is it okay for them to take all the resources in our land, destroy our homes, and leave us with nothing?' But people think they are going about trying to buy off individuals rather than dealing with the whole community as one. People suspect Nwokwe is Company's inside man, although he denies it.

"Others suggested we accept the money and buy cows with it and share among everyone for the festival. Whether we accept their terms is another matter. Someone cautioned them to bear in mind that it is the devil we are dining with here; we should therefore use a long spoon. These people have government on their side. They look like they are asking us, but they are not; they prefer to indulge us, at least. If any commotions come out here, then you will see who will come to battle. Everyone here knows you cannot fight government. No medicine can kill government. They will burn a holy shrine and go scot-free: something an ordinary person would do and not last the hour without falling down dead.

"Are you asleep?" Paul asked.

"No," Ajie replied, "I'm listening."

There was a faint distant drumming from the night. It could have been coming from another village, although as Ajie slid toward sleep, the drumming advanced and retreated, as if emanating from the farthest quarters of Ogibah or close to his window or the room next door, where Bibi was asleep.

Ajie had barely set eyes on Bibi throughout the day. They separated each time they came to Ogibah: They became boys and girls, each doing his or her own thing. Bibi had come in sometime that afternoon to ask Ma for a George wrapper and scarf for a dance practice she was taking part in. She had beads around her left ankle and on her wrists, and she had applied talcum powder all around the length of her neck and on the top of her chest and back. She would have looked really idiotic had they not been in Ogibah.

Did someone give birth? Ajie wanted to ask, but didn't. He would have heard the singing if there were a newborn. The showering of powder, the party of family and friends singing, dancing, and ringing bells from one end of the village to the next was always a rowdy affair.

"I am organizing a sports competition tomorrow," Bibi said to Ajie. "But you have to register if you want to participate." With her head-girl initiative, she had formed a committee of organizers and given leadership posts to some. "It's for both boys and girls," Bibi added before Ajie could say he wasn't interested.

The distant drumming of the night persisted, and Ajie thought he could make out voices, but he couldn't tell if it was just his own mind already in the zone, tilting on the edge of sleep, and conjuring up things. There were the three of them, Ajie thought, Paul, Bibi, and him. Before the beginning of his memory, which was to say from the beginning of this life, there had always been the three of them. Paul and Bibi were the first people he saw, the first he touched. Everything he resented and liked, everything he knew, thought, and felt, his smile and the angry pounding in his veins, were all from them, and now, for the first time, taking notice of this made him feel incredibly lonely. The sort of lonely feeling that Bibi would have been tempted to slap out of him. Just the kind of thing that would have made Paul look at him in his usual bemused way and say,

"My friend, what are you saying? Please be serious." But he sensed it that night, it hung about the room, the feeling that things may not always be like this, that they would one day grow up and live across town from each other, like Ma and her cousin Auntie Julie, or even die, like all of Bendic's siblings, whom he hardly ever spoke of.

The distant drumming had stopped. Paul turned over and mumbled something in his sleep, and Ajie was sure he could hear Bibi softly breathing from the room next door.

There is a house on the left corner of the square. If you are walking from Mercury Super Store, it's the first thing you will see. It's built of red brick and has wooden windows that open outward. There is a high veranda and there are five steps you have to climb to get to it. Beside this house, there is a path wide enough for a car to drive along.

Paul and Ajie turned left onto this road, and the sun was high, but the cotton trees that lined the path shielded them. They walked past Nwube's house, which had a stick barring the entrance to the narrow walkway. There was pounding coming from Nkaa's house, and the voices of women were loud and indistinct. Nkaa was a hunter, famed for killing three buffaloes in his lifetime, before buffaloes became extinct in Ogba land. People said that the buffaloes got offended and left due to the inhospitality shown them. Nkaa paid the price for hunting down these great beasts with his lack of children. Buffaloes, it was said, had strong spirits.

Here is the house Charlie built. The house his son now lives in since Charlie died. Ajie never met Charlie, but there was a popular ballad about him and his wife, Opi, that had endured.

Opi had refused to let Charlie have the chicken gizzard, which was a part reserved for the man of the house. The chicken thighs were the man's portion; the chicken bottom was his, too; so were the kidneys and the breasts. Opi, as it turned out, had developed a ruinous taste for gizzards and simply dished them out for herself all the time. These were the facts of this notorious domestic dispute. "What?" the final line of the ballad inquired. "Opi, what wrong did Charlie do to have married you?"

"Wait!" Someone was shouting and running toward them. "Wait." It was Ossai, Ajie's friend. "I went to your house to look for you, but you were not there. Someone said they saw you near Mercury. Where are you going?"

"We are going to see Boy in Obigwe," Ajie said.

"Do you want to come with us?" Paul asked. "We'll drive to Omoku. Boy's cousin has a party."

"I'll come," Ossai said, and fell in line with them as they walked along. "There is going to be trouble in town today," he continued, still breathless from his running.

Company had decided to give all of Ogibah a gift of twenty cows for the New Yam Festival. This morning two trucks drove into Ogibah with the cows and parked on the road beside Nwokwe's house. There was already fighting among the OYF. Some of the members thought the gift should be returned right away, that Company had ignored what Ogibah was talking about and instead had brought gifts to win them over. Other members thought it was stupid to return the gifts, it was a fine gesture, there was no point in being so extreme. Other people were wondering why the truck was parked in front of Nwokwe's house instead of in the square. Who apart from Nwokwe was consulted about the gift? Fighting had broken out that morning. Nwokwe's son, Ogbuku, had a third of the

OYF with him. If these old men wanted to talk forever, they could go ahead, but before sunset, there would be the smell of burning meat in the air.

Ossai had given them a detailed account of the morning skirmish when they finally hit Uhwo. "Morgan sent a message to Ogbuku saying that if any of the cows' blood dropped on Ogibah soil tonight, human blood would drop, too."

Uhwo was a vast spread of wiry grassland that stretched from Ogibah to Obigwe. Ma said Uhwo was an anomaly: a Sahel-like grassland that had no business being in a rain forest. Bendic said it was possible Uhwo was a desiccated river from hundreds of years ago. It still flooded often, and the soil was an ashy clay that didn't support much farming; it was a hot shrub steppe teeming with rodents and small lives. Animals came there to graze. It was there, by that tree, that Nkaa crouched in wait all night for a herd of buffaloes he had been tracking for weeks.

Each time Nkaa cut down a buffalo, the whole village came out to celebrate his kill. A medicine man would be sent for from an Ekpeye village, because Ekpeye people, it was believed, had strange and powerful medicines. As the buffalo was being flayed, torn apart, and disemboweled, the medicine man would take Nkaa to a hut to prepare his body against the attack of the buffaloes. That same night Nkaa would be escorted straight to his mother's people.

Late in the deep dark, buffalo cries would be heard. A herd of them would gather at Nkaa's door and weep all night. Why had he taken their brother? Why had he taken their mother? And if Nkaa had a pregnant wife at the time, the very next morning, she would see blood. After he killed his third buffalo in '82, his mother begged him to leave the creatures alone.

She wanted to have a grandchild from him before going to her grave.

They reached Boy's house and went in through the back door. Paul looked at his watch and said it was one-thirty and that they were just in time. Boy was already dressed. "Look at my Port Harcourt boys!" he shouted when he saw his visitors. "Look at my boys from Port Harcourt!" He shook hands with Paul and asked how he was doing. Some children sitting on the ground stopped their play to watch the new arrivals. Boy was about eighteen but always treated Paul like his mate. He liked to take them places whenever they came to the village. He would brag about them to friends. His first and only time in Port Harcourt, he had come with his mother to spend the weekend with the Utus at 11 Yakubu. Boy's mother had brought them a bunch of plantains, groundnuts, and palm kernels as gifts, and Bendic and Ma had said to her, "Oh why do you worry yourself so much." Boy had spent the weekend learning to play Nintendo games with Paul. When Bendic took them to Chanrai's and asked them to pick whatever they wanted, Boy didn't know what to pick; he didn't know if he wanted anything. Later he told Paul and Ajie that Chanrai's was like abroad, and was it the American man at the counter who owned the shop? Paul told him Jaysil wasn't the owner of Chanrai's, although someone in his family was, and that they were from India, not America.

The party in Omoku wasn't really happening, at least not yet. It was only three in the afternoon, and there was music coming from the room Boy led them to. It was dark inside, and Ajie had to squint to see the two people who were sitting on the bed. The stereo speakers were set on the floor, and Ajie could feel the vibration coming from the thumping of the music. Boy shook hands with the two boys sitting on the bed and told them these were his cousins. One boy stood up lazily and said welcome to them. He left the room and returned with four drinks, which he dropped on the floor beside them and nodded at Paul. He left the room again for a long time. He ushered in two girls when he came back in. "Have a seat," he said to them, and they sat down awkwardly on the bed beside Paul.

Later, Ajie heard Boy saying to the girls that Paul had come from Port Harcourt. One of the girls wore a blue cotton blouse with a red rose drawn over her bosom. She had a print wrapper around her waist and wore rubber slippers. Her face was white with talcum powder, and she looked like she would rather not be in the room. Her friend was chatting with Boy's friend. Chaka Demus & Pliers came through the speakers, chanting "Water Bam Bam"; the girls spoke quietly among themselves and then stood up and began to dance. They held each other's hands and moved to the beat. Boy went to the door and beckoned to Ajie. When Ajie stood up, Boy beckoned to Ossai, too, and they both followed him out of the room.

It was already dark when they got back to Ogibah. The air was thick and muggy and filled with the smell of roasted meat. While approaching from Uhwo, Ogibah was drenched in a shifting half-light that gave it the feel of an abandoned village. A place ruined, sacked, and set ablaze by an army from far away, carting away treasures, leaving behind the dead and the dying, and some livestock to roam the empty streets. Ajie heard the sound of pounding as they neared Nwube's house. There were a few bright stars and a quarter moon in the sky. Palm trees in the far distance stood away from each other, and beyond, beside Base Camp, the rushing red flames of flaring gas licked the sky.

Bibi was downstairs by the tank with her friends. "Ma and Bendic have been looking for the two of you. Where did you go?" she asked, sounding ominous. "They are upstairs, you better go and see them now." Her friends had stopped talking, waiting for Bibi to finish, and she fully occupied this space they had given her. The girls seemed impressed both by her command of English and by the authority in her voice. Paul and Ajie walked past without much of a response.

Upstairs, Ma looked at them and said, "Ah, you are back. Where have you been?" Then she looked away from them and continued talking to Bendic. When she glanced back and saw they were still standing there, she said, "Your food is on the kitchen table," and as they left the parlor, her eyes followed them. "Ajie, have you had a bath today?"

"Yes," Ajie replied, angry that Ma had singled him out to ask that question. They went to the kitchen, brought their food down, and sat on the dwarf kitchen stools to eat. They had not thought much of the smell of burned meat in the air when they first neared the village. They had not remembered or thought of the ten cows Ossai had talked about in the morning. Twenty cows that were brought in two trucks, a gift from Company to all of Ogibah as a gesture of goodwill for the festival. This gesture that had caused such ruction that morning. "We do not want their disgusting gift! They can't buy us from ourselves." "But why should we reject a gift during our festival?"

Morgan threw Nwokwe on the ground, and Nwokwe's son ran in for a machete and had to be restrained, and the warning cry, "*Otchu! Otchu!* Murder! Murder!" ripped the air.

Paul and Ajie did not know the details of how and why the

uproar was calmed, how it came to be that the cows were killed and shared among all the families in the village. If any portion was set aside for Bendic, it did not get into his house; it did not boil in Ma's pot.

Paul and Ajie finished their food and went to their room and then fell asleep almost immediately, until Ossai came to wake them up when it was time for *Ntitroegberi.*

The path to Nkaa's house was narrow and crowded by trees. Paul carried a flashlight so they could see where they were stepping. They walked in single file—Paul in front with the flashlight, Ajie in the middle, and Ossai behind. Nkaa was now the oldest man from their *Onubobdo,* so it was his duty to do the narration that night. For Paul and Ajie, this would be their first time to hear him tell the stories. They had always enjoyed how Okposi told the story of their ancestors' arrival at Ogba land— although the story was the same, each time it sounded different from Okposi's mouth—but he had recently died under the knife of a surgeon while having his appendix removed at the General Hospital in Omoku.

By the time Paul, Ajie, and Ossai arrived in Nkaa's front room, there was hardly any space left for them to sit. There was some shuffling about before Ajie and Ossai found a place on the floor to crouch, and Paul stood leaning on the wall beside them. The boy sitting in front of Ajie smelled of palm-kernel oil. He soon fell asleep and his head began to tilt slowly backward, and each time, just when Ajie thought to slap him awake, the boy caught himself with a quick jerk of his lolling head and then looked around, ready to refute anyone who accused him of dozing off.

There was a stir when Nkaa walked into the room. There was hardly enough passage for him to get to his seat, and the movement of people making space for him upset the sitting arrangement on the floor. This worked in some people's favor; Ajie tapped Paul on the leg and motioned for him to sit on the floor beside him. Nkaa cleared his throat and immediately began a call-and-response song. Ajie saw Bibi come in with two of her friends. She looked around, her eyes searching, and then she walked toward the left of the room, where some of her friends who'd arrived earlier had kept a place for her on a bench.

CHAPTER EIGHT

The school gate was made of wrought iron, freshly painted green. New block work was in progress to replace the barbed wired fencing. Students in checked red uniforms dotted the side roads and parking lot. Ma sat alone in the back of the car as it approached the barrier. Marcus wound down the window to talk to the security man at the gate; he was dressed in a navy blue polyester uniform and held a stick in his hand. The man looked into the car, nodded at Ma, and then waved them on.

Visiting-day regulations required that students remain in their dorms, carrying on as normal, until their parents arrived, at which point a staff member on duty at the gate would send for them. But it was nearly noon, and prefects ignored their duty, rules slackened, and loitering became the order of the day. Those who were hopeful their parents would visit sneaked about, scanning the gate for cars that looked like their parents'. Some attached themselves to friends whose parents had already arrived, heading down together to be introduced—as seatmates, bunk mates, dorm mates, new best friends—eager for a taste of some home cooking.

Paul sat with his friends on a windowsill in the senior class-room block, with a clear view of the gate. When he saw the Peugeot 504 come through the gate, he didn't check to confirm the plate number: He knew too well that blue metallic sheen of the chassis, the particular glint of the windshield, and on which corners of it the insurance stickers were stamped. He snapped his fingers at a passing junior boy whom he ordered to go fetch Ajie at once. "If you divert, you are dead."

"Yes, Senior." The junior boy scampered off.

Paul and Ajie soon joined Ma where the car was parked beneath a whistling pine tree by the science laboratories.

"Look at the two of you!" Ma gasped in horror. "You are all necks." She drew Paul close, feeling his body to see how much weight he had lost.

"Ma, stop." Paul laughed, trying to pull away.

"You are all bones," she declared. "Ajie, are you skipping meals? Or is it that they are not serving proper food in that dining hall?" She turned around. "Marcus, come and look at my children o!" Paul and Ajie greeted Marcus.

"Madam, it's growth," Marcus said playfully. "They are stretching out, that's why they are thin."

"This stretching is too much," Ma said, searching her children's faces and bodies with her eyes. "Let this school not kill my children for me, please."

They threw open all four doors of the car to allow for a good supply of breeze. It was the second week in February, and here in the hilly lands of the east, the receding harmattan season had left the air dry and balmy. The soil was a stony red. The generator house stood at a remove from them, and behind it was a stretch of field that was stopped by the barbed wire fence. From where they sat, they could see the Enugu–Port Harcourt Expressway and the vast cashew plantation that stretched far and wide on the other side of the road.

Ma served and passed the food to them, leaning into the car from where she stood by the trunk. Spicy fried rice with diced carrot, green peas, chopped liver fried to a crisp, and stewed chicken. Marcus insisted Ma serve him only a small portion so he didn't doze off at the wheel from a heavy stomach.

They all dug in.

"Why did Bendic not come?" Paul asked.

"He probably has a court case in Lagos or something," Ajie informed Paul, teeth clenched, eyes squinting as he chewed a piece of chicken thigh.

"Your father is resting," Ma said. "The doctor asked him to take some days off and relax at home."

"Some days off? Is Bendic sick?" Paul asked, looking at Ma.

"He just needs rest; you know how your father carries on with work," Ma said. "Dr. Idoniboye said he must slow down a bit, reduce his movement a little."

"I can't imagine Bendic obeying any instruction like that," Paul said.

Ajie thought of Bendic lying in bed compulsorily. Faceup, hands by his sides, not moving or turning, just lying there inert for a whole week and then getting up to go about his business when the time had been served fully.

"At home or in the hospital?" Paul asked.

"At home now," Ma replied, a little reluctant. "He stayed in the hospital for three days first. He's fine, don't worry your heads."

She didn't tell them that Bendic had slumped in his office one afternoon and been rushed to the hospital, that he had remained unconscious for two days before he came to. She didn't tell them about the series of tests they had to run; about carrying him back and forth between their home and Braithwaite Memorial because that was the only hospital in Port Harcourt that was equipped to carry out the tests. Then there was the weeklong wait for the results. She didn't tell them how she had prayed, really prayed, for the first time in a long time; how she had felt she was standing on a precipice, a raging wind at her back, the dark bottomless unknown before her. They would never know of the promise she made to God at that moment, and then to herself, to nature, to the universe, to whatever was good and great out there, that if only things could turn out right, please let this thing turn out right.

She looked up at her children and said, "Your father wrote you letters, but finish your food first."

Marcus looked back and said, "Look at all the food still on your plates. Paul, Ajie, what's happening? Quick quick, there's still more food in the cooler."

For afters, there was a fruit cocktail: pineapple, paw-paw, and mango, sliced and swimming in the juice in a big bowl. The ripe, sweet smell of the mango filled the car, and two flies buzzed about. Paul held his palm up, aiming to hit as the flies came his way. They buzzed and zigzagged about the car, bumping into the windows as Marcus beat the air with a newspaper, and then they escaped.

"I went to see Bibi last weekend," Ma said. "She was selected to represent her school in an all-girls cantata."

"Really, where are they playing?" Paul asked.

"Ilorin."

"Wow," the children chorused.

"Is she flying there or going by bus?" Paul asked.

"They are flying," Ma replied.

"That's all we will hear about when we go back home," Ajie said. "Bibi will talk about it so much, like she is the first person in the whole world to have ever entered an airplane."

"Jealousy!" Paul laughed as if he weren't also secretly coveting Bibi's airplane adventure.

"Is she still playing that instrument, what is it called?" Ajie asked to lower the tone.

"Oboe, yes, she is playing two solos," Ma replied.

"Shitted!" He cupped his mouth with his left hand.

"What type of language is that?" Ma threw him a disapproving glance and leaned forward to the glove compartment to get a toothpick.

"Bibi shouldn't be doing things like that," Paul joined in.

"What do you mean, Paul?" Ma challenged. "She plays the oboe well."

"Ma, just hear how it sounds: oboe," Ajie said.

"Like 'oh no.'" Paul laughed. "Why can't she just play the trumpet or drums?"

"Trust Bibi to pick an odd instrument," Ajie said.

"Her music teacher is very proud of her, and so is her principal. You haven't been chosen yet to represent your school in anything."

"Shitted. Ma, that's harsh," Ajie said, laughing. "Still, Bibi is running down our family name."

"Paul, what's this 'shitted' your brother keeps saying?"

"Don't mind him, Ma. It's just silly junior boys' slang."

"What is wrong with it?" Ajie said.

"Is that what we sent you here to learn?" Ma's voice had risen to a scold. She turned to face Ajie properly. "Let this be the first and the last time I will hear it from your mouth, you hear?"

Having sufficiently flattened the mood and looking for a way to revive it, she opened a bottle of Sprite and passed it to Paul. "Which one do you want?" she asked Ajie.

"Fanta," Ajie said.

After they had eaten, they sat back, watching other families. Marcus put on the radio and turned the knob until it caught a station playing a reggae tune—Majek Fashek singing "Send Down the Rain," which at that moment seemed fitting. Soon it was time for Ma and Marcus to drive back to Port Harcourt.

Ajie rummaged through the bag of provisions Ma had just handed him. Paul was looking through his bag, too. Ma gave them their letters from Bendic and told them to send their replies once they could. "Do you still have stamps left? I should have gotten you some more, completely forgot."

"They sell stamps in school," Ajie said, "but I still have about six left."

"You people shouldn't forget my birthday-o," Paul said. "You can send a money order. Just a suggestion. And yes, tell Bendic to expect my letter."

"I will tell him," Ma said. Regarding Paul's birthday, she said they could have a party, by the grace of God, when they returned for midterm break or long holiday. Ajie thought Ma was being rather agreeable, so he said he wouldn't mind if they threw a party for him as well. Ma asked Paul how he was coping with being deputy head boy, and Paul said there was really nothing to it. Ma looked at Ajie to comment, and Ajie looked back at her and said nothing.

"We've begun heats for the interhouse sports competition." Ajie perked up. "I'm marching."

"That's good," Ma said, then turned the other way. "What about you, Paul?"

"Paul is in the senior boys' four-by-hundred relay. He's throwing the javelin, too," Ajie said.

They drove to the entrance of the dormitory area and the

boys got out of the car, stood together, and waved to their mother and Marcus, who honked twice as the car rolled off. They watched as the car went down the sloping road toward the classroom area, passing by the staff rooms, the teachers' tearoom, the laboratories, the library, the fields, and the parking lot slowly emptying of cars. The blue Peugeot 504 paused by the gate for a security check, and then, with the orange light indicating left, disappeared into the evening mist.

Ajie did not read his letter until after dinner. He put the envelope carefully in between his introductory technology textbook as the bell rang for night prep. The handwriting seemed particularly formal, but it was one he was used to.

My dear Ajie,

I'm sorry I couldn't come with your mother for your visiting day as I promised. The doctor has advised me to take some rest so I'm staying back this time and will hear all about how you and your brother are doing when your mother and Marcus return.

I hope you've adjusted well now to life in the dormitory. It can't be easy, but I know you are tough enough to survive it. I hope your brother is showing you the ropes so you avoid getting into too much trouble.

How is your math?

Remember what we agreed you should do when someone tries to annoy you. The backward count always works. Take it slowly from 100, and before you know it, you will think of something better than to lash out. Don't be afraid to report anyone who is bothering you. Did you write to your sister?

I hope to be going to Abuja in a few weeks. I have

*been selected, among other people in the state, as part
of a committee to discuss revenue allocation with the
government. If you ask your brother, he might be able to
explain to you.*

Write to us.

Your affectionate father,

*P.S.: Mr. Onabanjo has said he doesn't see you enough.
He is your guardian—why are you avoiding him? He
sends for you and you don't go. Please, report to his office once every week, Fridays preferably. Let him know
how you are doing. I will call him.*

The newspaper selection at the school library did not run
any story about Bendic's trip to Abuja and what he said in those
meetings. Neither Paul nor Ajie stumbled across their father's
name while flipping through the papers that were brought daily
to the large *reference* table in the library, but what did it matter,
anyway?

The newspaper front pages in the months that followed carried stories about revenue allocation, think tanks set up for
community development, and governors cutting ribbons for
commission projects with much fanfare.

In Ogibah, Nwokwe's son began preparing to run for local
government chairman. He had been a secretary in OYF, and
many people suggested he run for a councillorship position in
the local government first, but he refused. He had the backing
of his father for the top job.

Some people would later say the trouble all began when
Nwokwe made his son run for office; they said after then that

things were never the same in Ogibah. Some said it was all the fault of Company; that it began in those early years when they first arrived in their coveralls and jungle boots. Others said the trouble in Ogibah had nothing to do with any of those but started from when human beings decided to live together in a community, knowing all the while they were prone to savage betrayals, filled with the desire to conquer each other, yet making no sufficient safeguards against these. Application Master declared it was greed, Nwokwe's and his son's greed, and that was all.

CHAPTER NINE

Bibi loved opening letters. Like all girls, she loved secrets—having, hiding, and revealing them only in exchange for more dangerous ones. She grew tall in the year after she entered secondary school, and during that holiday she befriended, for a brief time, a round-faced girl who had turned up on their street. A girl from number 17. She was one of Chief Wokoma's children but had lived since birth with her mother, who from the start refused to share a roof with Chief Wokoma and his other three wives.

The girl sauntered through the gate one Friday afternoon, and it was Bendic she met first, sitting on the veranda and taking some fresh air while everyone else was in the parlor. Bibi had received a letter from her best friend that afternoon and, after reading it in the privacy of her room, colonized a big portion of the dining table, where she sat to compose her reply. Paul needed much space on the dining table, too, because his new Sony Walkman had dealt him some treachery, cutting a few of his favorite cassette tapes. Paul had been bent over all afternoon, undoing the tiny screws on the cassette, then unwinding the spool of glistering brown tape to locate the severed parts. He sweated in the warm air of the parlor and his frustration mounted. Bibi refused, even after Paul's suggestions, to use the lower center table in the seating area to do her letter, so a silent war raged on the dining table as they bore down on their respective tasks with unflinching focus.

Ajie sat on the sofa opposite Ma and hoped power would be restored. Even though the TV stations wouldn't have come on yet, at least there would be that muted vibe, the hum of electricity waiting in sockets, making the fridge breathe, and at least the ceiling fan would be spinning and blowing air across the room. Ma was asleep, her head thrown back as she let out air softly through her parted lips.

"Good afternoon, sir." The girl's voice came from outside. Bibi continued being busy with her letter writing; Paul was now using a Bic pen to roll in his metallic chrome cassette.

"Oh, I see," Bendic was saying to the girl. "You are Chief Wokoma's daughter?"

"Yes, sir." She was now on the veranda with Bendic. "I'm his daughter. My brothers said there is someone in this house I can play with."

"Yes, yes, there are," Bendic said. "My children are inside. Bibi," he called out, "Paul, Ajie."

"What's your name?" Bendic asked.

"Wendy," she replied.

"Wendy."

"Nwenenda," the girl said by way of explanation, "but everyone calls me Wendy."

Ajie stood by the window and watched the girl in her short dungarees and white T-shirt. And then she walked into the parlor. "Good afternoon, Ma," she said loudly, startling Ma out of her afternoon dream.

"Mm-hmm," Ma mumbled, smacking her lips and swallowing. "Afternoon, my daughter, how are you?" She squinted and smiled as if she had any idea who the girl was.

"I am fine, thank you, Ma," Wendy said, and Ma turned back toward the dining table to see where Paul and Bibi were; in her groggy state, she was assuming the girl was one of Bibi's friends whom she should know.

"How are your parents?" Ma found herself asking. Bibi left the dining table and came over to Ma and Wendy. Paul had suspended his tape rolling and was watching.

"What were you doing?" Wendy asked, smiling at Bibi as if to say, *Let's just accept that we are good friends already.* Her eyes were scanning the framed photographs on the wall as she and Bibi walked back to the dining area. "My name is Wendy."

Ajie was watching Paul watch Bibi and Wendy. Apart from her sky-blue short dungarees, Wendy had everything else to match: white T-shirt, white sneakers, white socks, and white wristwatch strap.

"Bibi," Bibi replied. "My name is Bibi. I was just replying to a letter from my friend." She pulled out one of the dining chairs for Wendy, but the two of them just stood behind the chairs for a moment, and right then Ajie would have loved to call Bibi by her full name; he would have loved to cough out, "Edobibi!" in his thickest Ogba accent, anything that might mar the sweet first impression Bibi seemed so bent on making. He would go on to explain to Wendy, who would be manifestly appalled by such an uncool name, "She was born in the year our house in the village was completed. Her name simply means *a place to live,*" and then it would be left to Ma to raise her voice and say, "No. *Home.* It means *home.*" But anyway, Bibi beat him to it. "My brother Paul"—she gestured toward Paul, and then turning the other way—"Ajie, my kid brother."

Kid stung him. The way Bibi delivered it, knowing exactly what she was doing and counting on him to endure the slight until at least the visitor was gone. Ajie snorted, hissed, and swayed in resentment, but no one noticed. Wendy nodded coolly at Ajie, and although Paul was right before her, she waved her fingers *hi-yaa* and immediately turned to Bibi as if there were something they had to discuss.

"Bibi, won't you offer your friend something?" Ma asked. "I think we have some soft drinks in the fridge."

Wendy shook her head at Bibi and winced in a big-girl sort of way, *Don't bother.*

"So you are always writing letters to your friends. Who is this one to?" Wendy asked.

"Atinuke, my best friend. She lives in New Bussau," Bibi said, shifting the writing pad away

"Where is that?"

"Niger State. It's where you have the Kainji Dam. I think her father works in NEPA."

"Hmm, okay."

"I just received her letter today. I wanted to reply at once," Bibi said. Everyone in the parlor was listening to the two of them, and their chat took on an air of play rehearsal.

"You live at number seventeen, right?" Paul asked.

"Oh, yes." Wendy turned to face him, looking a little surprised that Paul was there at all.

"We know your brother Wobo," Paul said.

"Oh, no, my brothers." Wendy rolled her eyes toward the ceiling. "They frustrate me. Why do you think I left to come here?"

"What did they do?" Bibi asked.

"I don't know. They are all much older than me, and they are just mean and boring. Jesus." She sighed and then looked at Paul. "What class are you in?"

⚔

Two weeks later, on a moderately warm Friday evening at about five-thirty, Wendy went berserk with rage and called Paul a "stupendous ignoramus" and Paul yelled, "You nematode!" in her face.

"Take this fake rubbish away." Bibi shoved the BMX bicycle back at Wendy.

Wendy held on to her bike with one hand and stepped in front of Bibi, stared her down, moving her eyes up and down, up and down, and then hissed, "We shouldn't even be breathing the same air. You scruffy thing."

"That's enough, now. Take your bike and go." Paul put himself between the two girls.

"Ask your father to buy you your own bicycle," Wendy shouted as she rolled off.

"Ask your father to stop picking you things off the dump," Bibi shot back. At which point Ajie thought she deserved a round of applause, but his knee was scraped and still hurting from the altercation that had preceded the ongoing fallout.

An hour before, they were all laughter, shrieks, and shouts as Paul gave Wendy a crossbar down the street with Bibi and Ajie running behind them. Bibi then asked to have a go and pedaled up and down the street while Ajie, who couldn't ride properly, was counting on Paul to give him a hand. When Bibi got off the bike, Ajie assumed it was his turn next and asked Wendy if he could ride, but she refused: "I can't let you practice with my bike, you will spoil it and my father will be angry." She pedaled off.

Paul told Ajie to relax, he would ask her himself, but Ajie went and stood by the dogonyaro trees, watching them, keeping a decided distance so as to feel lonely enough, and imagining how one day the girl would be knocked down by a bigger, faster bicycle or an okada and how he would not care when she returned from hospital on crutches, in bandages and casts.

"Don't worry, Ajie, come." Bibi beckoned to him in high spirits. "I'm sure she was just joking."

When Wendy cycled back to where they stood, Paul asked if she could let Ajie learn to ride, and Wendy pursed her lips and reluctantly stepped aside. Twilight had descended in an instant and clothed the trees in shadows. "Steady," Paul said to Ajie as he got on the bike gingerly. Paul touched gently on the handlebars to keep them steady.

"Don't pedal too fast," Bibi admonished, "just take it slow." Then she turned to Wendy. "I think he'll be fine, he won't spoil your bike." Bibi failed to notice the unyielding look on her friend's face. She couldn't see beyond her own excitement that her friend wasn't with her, so she just rubbed sand off her face and kicked her bathroom slippers to the curb and walked behind the bike as Ajie stepped, ever so gently, on his first pedals, Paul's hand still on the handlebar, Bibi following right behind. They were soon doing a quick walk, a jog, and then a sprint. Ajie was pedaling along all by himself. "Yeah!" Bibi threw her hands in the air. "We did it!" Ajie looked back and realized they weren't holding on to the bike anymore; he kept his feet working on the pedals—if he stopped stepping, he would fall, so he looked ahead and kept his frame steady. When he saw the pothole, he swerved and tried to return his hands to a straight position, but everything became wobbly and crazy and he saw himself going down in slow motion. *Kraap!* The bike scraped the tarmac. He tumbled off and fell flat on the road. His knee burned with pain. In a second, Paul was there, pulling him off the ground. "Ajie, Ajie, are you okay?" Bibi was looking at Ajie's bruised knee now, blowing air to soothe it, saying, "Sorry, it's only a scratch," and then looking at Ajie's face to confirm if she was right: *It's only a scratch, isn't it? Nothing is broken . . .* That was when Wendy walked up to where they were huddled together on the ground. She picked up her bike from the ground and checked to see if anything was damaged.

Paul was looking at her. "Sorry," he said, then looking back at Ajie, "he has wounded himself."

That was when the roaring came out of her: "I don't care! It's all your fault! Stupendous ignoramus!" Paul leaped to his feet, quivering with rage, and for a whole second there was no sound from him, then he screamed, "You nematode! Horrible creature, and you can go to hell with your bike."

Ajie got up and tried his leg out in a few steps, as if checking for damage. The security lights of the nearby compounds began to come on as Wendy walked toward her gate.

"Let's go home, don't mind her," Paul said, "she is a very stupid girl."

"No wonder her brothers hate her," Bibi added, but Ajie couldn't help feeling the heaviness that somehow he had ruined everything.

Bibi wrote a letter that night, under candlelight. She made several drafts and threw the old ones in the bin, crumpled up in a ball. She covered up the letter when anyone got close, as if shielding class exercises from a seatmate. "State secret," Ma said, and clicked her tongue."Mind your eyes, Bibi, that letter can wait till daybreak."

Bibi bent over it, perfecting all four pages of the final draft in her most careful handwriting.

She had no reason to suspect that anyone would salvage her discarded pages from the bin.

I think Paul has a girlfriend in school, she wrote. *I suspect it. I don't even know if she's fine since I haven't seen a picture, and my younger brother, Ajie, is being stingy with details. All I know is that she's a Hausa girl.*

You know our neighbor I wrote to you about in my last letter? Wendy. Hmm. Story is beginning to come out. She really liked Paul. I think they went to the abandoned trailer park not too far from the house to hang out and they kissed. I'm not too sure, but it's very likely.

Now, here is the gist. Paul took Ajie with him the next time he was supposed to meet her. I think he was feeling guilty because he kissed someone else when he has a girlfriend. Not sure . . . but you know me, my instincts are always right. I overheard something! I think Paul wanted Ajie to learn how to kiss from Wendy. My brothers are so weird. Anyway, the whole thing backfired. The girl got so upset she wouldn't let Ajie anywhere near her bicycle. She was just enduring Paul and me for half of one afternoon, and then she couldn't take it any longer and she exploded like a grenade.

What's happening with that Obinna boy? Is he still begging you?

My father and mother are going to America in two months' time. We are going to stay with Uncle Tam, who is not really our uncle but that is what we call him.

CHAPTER TEN

Ajie followed Paul into the yard. Abandoned trac-
tors were afield, overgrown by elephant grass and shrubs
of *awolowo*. Two or three earth tillers gathered rust, their
flattened tires sinking into the loam. A woman with a child
braced on her hip came out of a house on the far corner of the
compound and emptied a basin of wash water in front before
disappearing into the darkened passage. The windows of the
unplastered house were boarded up with planks.

"Ajie." Paul beckoned, stepping aside on the tiny path so his
brother could walk ahead as they made their way toward the
fence. Paul began to whistle. Everything was yellowy under the
November sun. The chill of the coming harmattan was already
in the breeze. Ajie looked at his feet and felt that he had applied
too much of the pomade. Grains of sand were stuck on his feet,
between his toes, and on his calves, courtesy of his flapping
oversize slippers.

"Can you jump?" Paul asked.

"Mhm." Ajie nodded confidently.

"Oh, look," Paul said, and walked off the path again and
onto the grass. "There is a hole in the fence. I didn't see that last
time. Let's squeeze through instead."

"Okay," Ajie said, disappointed. He had wanted to scale the
fence ever since Paul had suggested it was a nice shortcut from
the street behind their house to the barber. They didn't have

to walk on the road past Ikom Street all the way down to Sangana. They had gained ten minutes now, as the sound of traffic reached them from the road up ahead. Ajie followed his brother's blue T-shirt while they weaved through the bush, dwarfed by the tall grass. Startled dragonflies buzzed and darted.

They came out of the bush and walked toward a row of newly built shops. The first was a restaurant. A glass showcase arrayed with fried fish and skewered peppered beef was stationed right in front. A little board leaned on the legs of the showcase with a sign written in white chalk: *Better Isiewu inside*. The strong smell of the spiced goat meat came through the beaded curtain as they walked past. A dry goods store was next, with empty beer crates piled high on the veranda, nearly touching the ceiling. The third was a barbershop. Loud bumpy music came from inside.

Paul slid open the glass door and walked in like someone who was quite used to coming there. The posters on the wall were of American rappers and R&B stars in baggy jeans and shirts accessorized with big shoes, long neck chains, silver crosses, rings, and tall hair: Kriss Kross, Naughty by Nature, Boys II Men, Poison, MC Hammer, Bobby Brown, Da Brat.

The barber nodded at them as they took a seat. He was putting finishing touches on a customer's hair. "Two of you?" he asked.

"Yes," Paul said, "my brother will go first."

Ajie sat down. "Which number?" the barber asked him, motioning toward the picture catalog of numbered hairstyles stuck to the mirror. The barber wrapped tissue paper around Ajie's neck, then threw a blue cloth over him and clipped it at the back of his head with a plastic peg.

"Number eighteen." Ajie pointed at a box on the catalog.

The man in the picture had the sides of his hair cropped in a fading pattern that came together in a medium rise toward the center, and then on the left side, a slight part.

"Mandela." The barber nodded, approving. "Nice choice."

Ajie sat upright and grinned into the mirror. "You know the side part?" he asked, looking at the barber. "Can you do it on both sides?"

"What?" Paul stood up to look. "No. Ajie, you know Ma will be angry." Then to the barber, "Only one side part, please."

From the mirror behind, Ajie could see what the barber was doing to the back of his head. He watched as Paul bopped his head to the music and then the barber's hand covered his eyes so he couldn't see anymore. When the barber was done, he used his talc brush all over Ajie's neck and face, and afterward Ajie looked in the mirror, turning his head this way and that, squinting and at the same time gauging Paul's face for signs of approval. Paul gave him a thumbs-up and made to take his seat. Nothing, Ajie thought, would ever make him return to that other barber that Ma took him to at Mile 3 market, with his manual clippers that left faint zigzag lines on your head.

Ajie sat back on the padded bench as the barber began to work on Paul's hair. Paul explained to the barber carefully and in detail how he wanted his hair. Ajie heard Paul's voice without taking in the words. Paul touched the back of his head as he spoke, then the sides, brushing his temples in a way that might have meant something, and then looked up at the barber, who nodded as he sprayed the blade with a sterilizer, picked up the vial of blade oil, and applied it to the edge of the buzzing clipper, as if to say he already understood everything (*I know I know I know*) and that Paul needn't explain any further. He tested the sharpness of the blade on the back of his hand, then put the clippers to Paul's hair. The clipper hummed and crackled, and Paul's hair rolled off like a carpet.

A pair of brown leather shoes was set by the door when they got home. Application Master, who was half stretched on the sofa, was woken up by their entrance, and he exclaimed "*Swoy!* Look at these children.*" He looked them up and down the way grown-ups do when they think a child has grown way taller than they ever foresaw. "Come come come." He opened his arms to the both of them. His teeth were stained brown, his smile wide and childish. His *feni* tunic smelled of camphor. For Ajie, the smell of camphor was always linked to trunks, dark places, cockroaches, and death. Because it was the smell of people who came to visit from the village, it was also the smell of old people, and it was about old people that news often came.

Bibi and Ma came out of the kitchen. "Look at your hair!" Bibi exclaimed at her brothers. She turned, her eyes wide in consternation, toward Ma, hoping she would comment on the stylish haircuts. Ma paused for a moment to take in their new looks, and Ajie wasn't sure if it was displeasure on her face; if she approved, that didn't show, either, she just moved her lips in a way that said this could wait till later. "Application Master, do you want your drink now?" Ma asked. "Bibi." Ma gestured for her to go and get the drinks.

When Bendic returned, he changed from his work clothes and came out to the parlor to sit with Application Master. Bendic asked Paul to get him a glass of water, and Paul soon emerged from the kitchen with Bendic's beer mug filled and dripping with water. Bendic motioned for him to keep it on the side stool to his right. The wrapper on his waist was rolled up in a loose bunch in front so that the waistband of his Y-front briefs was visible.

Ma called Bibi to help with dinner and asked Paul to get the guest room ready. She wanted him to change the sheets and open the window to air the room.

Later that night, after dinner, they all sat outside because there had been a power outage and the air in the parlor had become warm and stifling. Bendic asked Ismaila to check how much diesel was left. "Maybe you can turn on the generator for an hour so we can watch the nine o'clock news."

"The buses all charged double fare today," Application Master said. "From Ogibah to Ahoada, and from Ahoada to Port Harcourt, they charged double the usual fare. As if what we used to pay was not already high enough."

"It is so o," Ma said. "We were lucky to be able to fill our tanks with petrol, but we couldn't find diesel for the generator."

There was speculation that tanker drivers were planning to embark on a strike the following week, so people flooded the gas stations, panic-buying and causing a shortage even before the speculated strike.

Bendic explained this to Application Master while the children waited, hoping to catch a hint of the matter that had brought Application Master from Ogibah. Ajie sat on a kitchen stool in the rough circle, certain the news would trickle out soon enough. Paul took off his shirt and fanned himself with it. Bibi had spread out a mat on the ground and was lying on it.

"It is unheard of," Ma said soon after, and Ajie saw the outline of her shoulders shrug in the moonlight. "Why should he send the police to arrest you?"

"Ogbuku has always been a bit stupid. And his father,

Nwokwe, sits back as his son misbehaves like this?" Bendic said. "Someone has to stop him before he goes completely mad. All that Company money he is eating has gone to his head. The fact that a fellow citizen can send the police to arrest another person is a different matter altogether."

"They call Ogbuku 'Chop-I-Chop' these days," Application Master said. During the campaign for the local government chairman position, his message to the Youth was that whatever he got once he was in office would not be for his pockets alone, that he was not the greedy type, whatever he could collect would surely go around. "You chop, I chop" would be his modus operandi. Not like the old-timers, who he said wanted to keep everyone away from the pot.

"I still don't see how that gives him the right to eat the money meant for renovation of the only school we have."

"It takes a certain originality to call that pitiful job he did an upgrade," Ma chortled. "Ultramodern, indeed."

"This petition I wrote that is running him crazy, he has no idea I can do worse than that. If I sit down properly and write a petition against him . . . eh?" Application Master sighed. "These young ones think that they can do as they like." He touched his breast pocket, but the pens that he always had clipped on weren't there.

A band of policemen had come into the village one morning and arrested four boys. Four boys they found sitting by the road near the empty market stalls. They shot them with Taser guns first to encourage their cooperation. Then they hit them with batons to make sure. By the time people arrived at the scene just after they had taken the boys away, they saw blood-stains in the sand.

Two weeks earlier, Application Master had written a petition against Chop-I-Chop, who was the current councillor for the ward and had his eyes set on becoming the next local government chairman. A contract had been awarded for new classroom blocks for the secondary school in Ogibah. Chop-I-Chop's company won the contract. The project was billed as an ultramodern learning center. In other words, it was six classroom blocks, complete with laboratories, staff room, library, and gatehouse. Many months passed before work began on the school site. The "ultramodern" project manifested as a three-classroom block with rough unplastered walls and floors, no ceiling, no staff room, no library, no laboratories. Once the roofing was done, pupils began to take lessons in the classrooms because the old block was overfull.

People grumbled: Chop-I-Chop could have followed the blueprint and built decent classroom blocks and still have made a killing from the contract. They summoned Chop-I-Chop to answer for himself at a youth meeting; he didn't bother to show up. He said the project had been inspected and the execution approved and commended by representatives from Company (who had awarded the contract as a community development project to soothe tempers frayed by the ongoing construction of the new pipeline). Why were they all going mental, Chop-I-Chop asked, about money that did not even come from their own pockets? He dismissed the elders' talks as the prattle of yesterday's men.

Application Master then wrote a petition against him to the local government chairman; copies of the petition were sent to the general manager of Company, to the manager of the department in charge of the inspection of the project, and finally, to the office of His Excellency, the governor of Rivers State.

When Chop-I-Chop got wind of the petition, he decided to go shake up Application Master a bit and make him withdraw his submission. Things could be kept quiet at this stage, so he went to the police station in Ahoada and had a little talk with the DPO. Two policemen in plainclothes were dispatched to do the job.

They enter the courtyard of the house and demand to see "Mark Alari, the owner of the house."

Application Master's sister in-law, who is in the out-kitchen frying *garri,* simply hollers over the hiss of the pan, "Who is asking? Who wants to see the man of the house?"

The two men march to the shed and speak to her tersely in English and order her to go find her brother-in-law.

She pulls wood out of the fire. "Just a minute," she says to them, "please, sit here and wait," and then hurries out. In no time, word goes around. Strange men called at Mark Alari's house, demanding to see him, they wouldn't say who they are. Mark is on his way back from Aduche's house when the message gets to him. He is told to keep a low profile until they find out who these men are. What do they want? The young men who have gathered wonder among themselves. People from out of town come here, demand to see a man without stating their mission? Oh, back in those days when Ogibah was Ogibah, such madness would not last a second.

Ogibah youth gather at once and march toward Mark's house. They find the plainclothes policemen sitting on a bench by the kitchen shed and begin to question them: "Who are you? What do you want?" But the men will not say. So they order the men out of the courtyard. They should detain these men. Who knows what they have come for. They look suspicious. They may be hired killers, but even hired killers should know better than to come into Ogibah like that.

A boy pushes one of the policemen. The man pushes back and tells all of them to back off. "We are police," the man declares. The crowd reels. Police? But the excitement in the air isn't about to cool off yet. "Show us your ID," they demand. "Why did you not say this? In fact, we do not believe you. Your ID cards may be fake. Okay, okay, tell us, policemen, what have you come for? What is your mission?"

They have come for Mark Alari, they say. They have come to take him to the station for questioning.

"Questioning for what? What has he done? Who sent you? Show us your arrest warrant. Don't think you can intimidate us. You must think we are uneducated. To arrest a man from his house, you need a warrant. Is that not what the law says? If you are real policemen, you must know that much, at least!"

"You are obstructing the course of justice," the policemen say. "You are standing in the way of the law."

"We will obstruct any obstructable," a boy shouts back at the policemen. It is getting dark now. Someone from the crowd makes a sudden lurch toward one of the men. The policeman turns around and grabs the nearest person by the neck. "Did I touch you?" the man asks him. "Take your stinking hands off me. You think police work is work?" The policeman's grip weakens. The man begins to slap the hand off; the crowd cheers. The policeman reasserts himself, tightens his grasp. His colleague has come to his aid, and the crowd closes in. Application Master watches from behind the crowd in a position that allows him a good view of what is going on.

Now enters Agility. He could be anything from seventeen

to twenty-four years old. He is an up-and-coming stalwart of Ogibah Youth Front, a mover and an agitator. He gave himself the nickname Agility and bears it with great confidence because, as he said, he looked up the word in the dictionary and was quite proud of the meaning. This boy breaks through the crowd and strides toward the policeman, who is still holding the man by the collar. Agility looks the policeman straight in the face and says in a firm voice, "Leave him." The policeman ignores him. Slap, slap, pull. Slap, slap, pull. A struggle ensues, and pretty soon everyone joins in.

Application Master raises his voice from where he stands. "Calm down, steady, steady, young men." He is going toward Agility to calm him when he catches a glimpse of something going up in the air. It is the form of a man: One of the police has been lifted bodily, flung up into the night air, and abandoned, like a sacrifice, and the crowd parts to allow him to land without impediment. He meets the ground with a clumsy thud. Everything goes quiet. There is something quirky about his heavy fall, the sound of corporal damage. He lies there, leg drawn up at the knee. "Maybe he has broken something," someone says, "a leg, his waist, his neck, his back." They move closer to the man and do not notice when the other policeman relieves himself of their company. Voices of caution rise from the crowd. "We warned you boys to let them go; whatever comes out of this, you will carry it on your own heads." "But who knows their mission," other voices counter. Someone goes close to the fallen man and prods him with a finger. He doesn't respond. A firmer prodding. Then all of a sudden the man leaps from the ground, grazes a finger on the ground, and disappears into the night.

"He has escaped! He has escaped!" they shout as they run toward the road, and then loud arguments follow.

Three days later, a police van arrives and carries four boys away. The whole village is being accused of violence against police on official duty, and Application Master is wanted for inciting the violence.

Bendic slapped his arm and yawned. Mosquitoes made faint noises, and stars had begun to appear in the sky. Ma looked up and said it would be a blessing if it rained tonight. "The heat is too much."

The tall plantain tree in the corner waved its arms and cast a shadow on the fence. In the moonlight, the shadow looked like a pregnant woman with two children by her side, waiting for a bus by the road. Ajie closed his eyes and opened them and the pregnant woman was still there by the roadside, waiting for a bus, with her two children by her side. A southwesterly wind blew and the tree shadow took the form of boats on water, boats with high masts and swollen sails, like the drawing in Ajie's Macmillan school reader, a drawing that had underneath it the caption: *A fleet of boats.*

"We will see what we can do tomorrow," Bendic said. "Once Marcus comes to work, we will drive together to Ifenwa's house. His brother knows the commissioner of police."

Ajie looked toward the gate, but it was buried in the half-dark. He could not make out Ismaila's small concrete four-cornered shed. He wondered what it would be like if policemen came banging on their gate, asking to see Bendic. Ismaila would assume they were robbers. He would bring out his bow and poisoned arrows and aim at the gate. Then he would order the intruders in that big voice of his to vamoose. That is what he would say: "Vamoose or I shoot! Move or I move you!"

NEPA had a change of mind and restored power. "Light has come," Bibi squealed.

The adults got up, and the children carried the seats as they all trudged back inside. A new energy was injected into their evening. It was not that late, just a little past nine o'clock. They caught the tail end of the news, which was followed by a government-sponsored program about skills acquisition projects for rural women.

Bendic thought aloud about what he had to do the next day. He had to send for Ifiemi, his secretary, so they could draft letters to different people who could influence things. If this whole business of police in Ogibah were nipped in the bud, the trouble could be stopped from escalating. It could be stalled for a while, but only for a while. At some point the wheels would go a full cycle. More trouble would erupt, and on such a large scale that it would be difficult to predict.

Bendic and Application Master did not know that this was just the beginning. There were no dead boys yet. No girls had been dragged into the bush. Graffiti was yet to appear on the walls of the secondary school saying, "Ogibah, Fear the Nigeria Police and Army." None of these things had happened yet. For now, some policemen had been assaulted, a few boys had been arrested as a consequence, and Bendic was doing his best to save the situation.

CHAPTER ELEVEN

Ifiemi, Bendic's secretary, arrived before nine the next morning and immediately converted the dining area into an ad hoc office. She mounted the Imperial 66 typewriter at one end of the oval dining table. An enormous dictionary was set to her left, the covers frail from regular use. A wooden ruler with smooth edges, correction fluid, thinner, pens (black, blue, and red), erasers, and pencils were all set within arm's reach. Bendic drafted the letters in longhand on foolscap paper, and Ifiemi typed them out on crisp white A4 sheets. Bendic then corrected the typed drafts with a red pen, after which Ifiemi retyped them. By noon they were almost done. Only a few final adjustments needed to be made, polishing the letter for a perfect tone. This time Bendic dictated what should be added, his sentences delivered in an even tempo, like someone reading Scripture aloud in a church.

The children sat on the veranda, and Bibi mimed Bendic's words, pretending she had glasses balanced on the bridge of her nose that she kept adjusting, looking up every now and then to stare at the camera like newsreaders who spoke with fake voices and shuffled their papers at intervals.

Bendic, however, didn't need to look up to any camera as he dictated to his secretary—although there was a time when he drifted off midsentence, his brows lifting over the frames of his reading glasses, as if to acknowledge someone waving in a crowd. Ifiemi's hands waited on the keyboard. An angel in a thundering white gown hurried past and made the kitchen door sigh. "Are you there?" Bendic asked, as if it weren't he who had drifted off.

Are you there? This was how Bendic sometimes called for attention. When thoughts crowded his mind and he couldn't call up which name belonged to which child, he simply said, "Are you there? Bring me a glass of water, please." The children imitated and used it on each other. Paul would say to Ajie, "Are you there? You have forgotten to tie your shoelace." "Are you there? Try and bring down your voice, you are shouting." It could be anyone's name. You poked the person in the side while asleep and called, "Are you there?"

Ajie would later feel this was a presage to Paul's disappearance, a sort of rehearsal they had been at all along. That each time they said it to Paul, they were alluding to his eventual disappearance. The time indeed would come when they would look over to his empty bed to poke a finger in the mattress, to ask the question with eyes, not words, and still be left with nothing.

Ifiemi, whenever she didn't follow any of Bendic's sentences, simply let her fingers hover above the keys, and Bendic, not hearing the click-clack, would look at her and then repeat the last sentence, adding emphasis, although the sentence itself would have changed—in detail, not in essence.

To His Excellency, Colonel Dauda Musa Komo,
Military Administrator of Rivers State

REQUEST FOR INTERVENTION IN THE
IMPENDING CRISIS IN OGIBAH COMMUNITY

Your Excellency,

Paul had salvaged one of the discarded drafts from the dustbin; he spread it out.

There was also a letter for the Divisional Police Office (DPO) at Ahoada.

This was not the first time Bendic was taking up matters with the authorities. Once he had taken the federal government to court. That was a story his children all knew to its finest details, even though none of them had been born at the time. There had been an explosion in an oil well near the farmlands in Ogibah, which left the area ankle-deep in crude oil, pervaded with the stench of rotten fish floating belly-up in the ponds, so Bendic took the government of the Federal Republic of Nigeria to court.

The Land Use Decree of 1978 that would make all previous landowners mere tenants of the state was still six years away. It would allow you to farm on your ancestral land and bury your dead, but should anything of value be found, your tenancy would lapse and how you were dealt with was entirely up to the government of the day.

In any case, after the explosions in Ogibah, Bendic sued the government, and the case slowly wound through the courts for two years, and then a verdict was delivered. Bendic lost. The story of the court proceedings had become something of a legend in Ogibah. Bendic stood as his own counsel after he fired his lawyer a few hours before the fourth court session, when it became clear that the lawyer had been bribed like the other one before him.

On that day, March 7, 1974, at ten A.M., Benson Ikpe, the counsel representing the federal government, rose in front of the high court to argue the government's position in the matter of *Benedict Awari Utu & Ogibah Community* vs. *Federal Government of Nigeria*.

Those present in the court said Bendic spoke for so long that his voice got dry and hoarse and the judge asked for a glass of water to be brought.

This was the part of the story Ajie liked best. He would imagine the courtroom. Where would Bendic be standing, being both counsel and plaintiff? In the witness box? The courtroom had a considerable number of Ogibah people. There were more than a handful who had never gone further than Elele before the start of this case months ago, but here they were in the serene expanse of Station Road in Port Harcourt, disgruntled but firm in their belief that justice would prevail. There were other people in the court: lawyers, all in black robes, adjusting their blond wigs to a cocky angle, their twig collars flapping out like gills. Representatives from Company sat in a single row in smart suits and spectacles—Ajie didn't imagine them turning up in coveralls, jungle boots, and hard hats. Some had been flown in from their main offices in Europe.

There was a court clerk as well, and orderlies with severe faces, in navy blue polyester uniforms, their shoes old but well blackened and shined. Over the sea of heads, benches, and wooden partitions sat the judge, chief goon, master of ceremonies. There was something celestial about the array.

Bendic was standing in the witness box. Sheaves and sheaves of documentary evidence he had amassed had been laid carefully in front of him. Photographs of swamplands and ponds covered in grease, ruined cassava farms burned to frazzle. When Bendic answered the questions he was asked, Ogibah heads nodded, and their hearts sighed in affirmation of the details of the disaster. Bendic spoke till his throat got hoarse, and Chief Goon sent an orderly for a glass of water. At this point, as the story went, clapping erupted among the Ogibah people in the courtroom; it could not be helped. Their man had spoken at such great length that water had to be brought for him. Chief Goon banged his gavel many times to calm the court and warned the people very seriously not to interrupt his court session again, else he would have no qualms holding the lot of them in contempt.

Of course, on the day the verdict was delivered, when Chief Goon put down the gavel for the final time, it was to rule against Bendic and Ogibah.

Mboy *ka* Israel was detained in court that day because he stood up, just before the judge finished reading out the verdict; he pointed at the judge and yelled, "You are a liar, and a thief! *Agbra awe eya!* Blind devil."

Ajie let the click-clack of Ifiemi's urgent fingers on the type-writer keys into his afternoon reverie. There was the sudden yet expected sweep of the carriage at intervals. The carriage return bell, the brisk rolling in of fresh paper. He thought about Israel's son, Mboy, who was held in the court jail for one night and didn't make it with the others on the bus back to Ogibah that evening. Ajie thought of the judge; he tried but couldn't muster hatred for him: At least he had the decency to allow a glass of water to be brought for a man who really needed it. But Ajie sensed his small feelings of gratitude to the judge were misguided. He would ask Paul what he thought. He counted on Paul's perspective to steer him in the right direction and maybe ignite some indignation in him.

Marcus and Paul were sent off with the letters in the morn-ing, and Paul sat in the passenger seat with the letters on his lap as they headed for the Rivers State Government secretariat.

CHAPTER TWELVE

The next day was a Sunday. Everyone was tired from staying up last night and didn't appreciate Ma banging on their doors at five-thirty.

"Paul, wake up, wake your brother!"

"Ajie!" Paul hissed and rolled over on his bed but did not get up. "Are you there?"

Ajie stretched and yawned, then got up slowly, feeling a little giddy from the already violent start of the day. There was no smell of frying onions and yam chips in the air, or of scrambled eggs with diced tomatoes. It seemed unfair to have to rush down a slice of bread and tea on a Sunday morning. It was like a reprise from term time: the hassle of school rising bells, running to the dining hall with plate in hand, dorm inspections, standing next to his bunk with the mattress dressed in white sheets while waiting for the incoherent housemaster, Mr. Ubani, to saunter through, randomly asking to see fingernails and teeth before running a finger across the top of lockers for dust.

"Get up for morning devotion." Ma's voice came from the passage, and Ajie could hear Bibi shut the door to her room as she made her way to the parlor. Paul was by the door, and Ajie got up and followed as they went to sit in the parlor.

Bendic did not join them for morning devotion. He stayed in bed a little longer than usual on Sundays, and Ma said it was important for their father to rest.

Bibi perched on the edge of her seat, her sleeping wrapper draped loosely around her from the neck down. The reading was from the Book of Genesis. Paul read the verses with his eyes half open; his voice had morning cobwebs in it.

Ajie sat erect, but his eyes were shut tight. Ma looked at him for a while. "Ajie!"

"I'm not sleeping," he said with his eyes still closed. "I'm trying to concentrate."

"Hmm!" Bibi sniggered. "Concentrate."

"Paul, please continue reading," Ma said, ignoring Ajie so they could get through with the devotion on time.

It was the story of Cain and Abel. The moral lessons could be anything from avoiding jealousy to making a worthy sacrifice to God. Cain offered his less than best to God, then got jealous and murdered his brother, Abel, who had given a worthy sacrifice. Ma facilitated these morning sessions, where everyone was encouraged to contribute, to ask questions.

"If Cain and Abel were the first offspring of Adam and Eve, and Adam and Eve were the first humans on earth, who then did Cain marry to father the rest of the human race? If Adam and Eve had other children later, that would mean he probably married his own sister?" Ajie had his hand on his chin, one leg drawn up on the couch. "Was that how they multiplied and replenished the earth?" He paused for a while, allowing space for thought and for the others to take in the cut of his inquiry. "That would just be disgusting," he concluded.

Paul hissed at him as he was saying the final word. "It's like you are going mad, Ajie." Bibi leaned back on her chair, unconcerned, the way you do when your advice and recommendations have been ignored. She once suggested to Ma that Ajie needed to be given five strokes of the cane every morning when he woke up, and that would set him straight, because, in her opinion, he was becoming something else these days.

Now, however, the word *disgusting* worked its way all over Ajie's face and projected across the room, all the way to the center table with the white lace cloth, to the tall room dividers where the silver JVC radio and TV sat, then whipped itself about the room and landed before them on the center table: *disgusting.*

Ma closed her Bible and placed it on an arm of her sofa; she took a deep breath and said, "Since you want to ask the question and then answer it yourself, I doubt there is anything left for anyone to add. Bibi, any contributions or lessons learned? Paul?"

After their morning devotion, the house bustled with activity. Ma was the army commandant and the children her new recruits.

"Go and have your bath now, the water is getting cold."

"Bibi, you cannot wear that skirt."

"Paul, please comb your hair."

All the while Bendic was in bed, sleeping or reading.

Ajie went into his parents' room to greet Bendic. The room was twice the size of the other rooms in the house, with its chest of drawers and standing mirrors framed in wood of mahogany tone.

"Come here," Bendic said, and Ajie sat beside him on the bed. "So your mother is taking you to church?"

Ajie nodded. His eyes strayed into the garden right outside the window. Ma grew everything from vegetables to herbs and flowers. Green peppers stood between corn and okra, and garden eggs next to her queen of the night.

It was Ma who first explained to Ajie, long before any of his primary school teachers did, the concept of photosynthesis.

Photosynthesis, she said to him slowly, was the process by which green plants produced their own food with the aid of sunlight. Ajie was intrigued; the words stuck to his mind indelibly. It was Ma who first told him the universe was billions of years old.

"But God made the world in seven days," six-year-old Ajie said, trying to wrap his head around the gaping discrepancy.

"That is true, too," Ma replied. "But the Bible has to be interpreted properly. People sometimes forget. You have to use the Bible to interpret the Bible. There is another verse that says, *One day unto the Lord is like a thousand years.* One day to God can mean millions, billions, of years for humans."

"Billions, Ma?" Ajie asked.

"Yes, billions. Science tells us our universe is thirteen point eight billion years old, nearly fourteen billion."

"Fourteen billion. How many zeros does that have?"

Ma smiled. "Nine. I can show you that later, Ajie."

Together, they carried out the experiment to prove that green plants would stretch in the direction of sunlight. Ma said creepers illustrated this point best, so they planted some bean seeds in a pot and placed it by the toilet window and observed how, days later, the stem stretched outside, toward the source of light. Ajie was only six, and this certainty of process, of order in nature, made him burn with a zeal that could rival that of any pioneer or prophet. He shoveled in the garden; he dug holes in the ground and dropped seeds in them and watered the spot until the plant sprouted. For two months he carried on until he lost interest in the work. The plants survived without his care for a while but eventually fared badly, and weeds ran amok.

"Quick, quick, everyone, get in the car," Ma called out. "Don't forget to bring a Bible with you." Paul wanted to change his trousers because he had just noticed the seams of the inner thigh had come loose. Ajie went into the bathroom and shut the door, and Ma flung a scarf at Bibi and then grabbed the car keys from the dining table. "Let me not wait for any of you," she threatened as she headed out to the car.

Since the start of that holiday, church attendance had become a regular thing in the household. Before then the Utus did only Christmas services or when someone invited them for a baby dedication.

Today they were honoring an invitation from one of Ma's colleagues who was having a Thanksgiving service after she miraculously survived a boat mishap on Bonny River. She was one of six survivors out of the initial twenty-two people who had embarked on the journey.

The church was packed full with people, and music came from a group of keen musicians who wore shiny blue satin tops and black trousers and skirts.

When the time came, Ma's colleague stepped out toward the stage. Ma nodded at Bibi when she asked if that was her colleague. The woman's blouse was the color of egg yolk and had a glazed sheen; her blue wrapper was heavily patterned with sequins, tiny circular mirrors, and dangling beads. As she walked toward the stage, another woman next to Ma shouted, "Hallelujah!" in anticipation of the well-known testimony. Ajie saw raised Bibles in the air, and there were scatterings of applause from different corners of the church. A lancing sound came from the microphone as one of the technical guys handed it to her. He then took it back, tapped on the mouthpiece one, two, gave a nod to the guys at the console, returned the mic to the woman, and then scurried away.

"Praaaaaaaa-ise the Lord!" She dragged out the words until the congregation was clapping again, standing and lifting their hands in praise, waving handkerchiefs in the air. "If it had not been for the Lord on my side," she charged, "I say, if it had not been for the Lord on my side, brethren, tell me, where would I be?" Her emotions got the better of her as she choked up, and some people in the congregation sighed. Ajie saw a tall man standing with his arms folded over his chest, his eyes fixed on the stage as if he had been struck by something. Ajie looked at him and thought that maybe he, too, had been saved from a boat mishap.

"Brothers and sisters, I don't know where to start." She took a deep breath to gather up her feelings, then began the story.

Paul nudged Ajie and told him to tap Ma. He mouthed some words to her and then stood up to go to the toilet. Bibi said she needed to go, too, and Ma refused and snapped, "Pay attention!" and Bibi just put her head down and continued doodling in her jotter.

"What I know is that one minute I was sitting on the boat, the next I was in the river. I am not the best swimmer in the world, but my God, the God who delivered the children of Israel from captivity, the God who rescued Daniel from the den of lions . . ." The whole church hall thundered with applause as the woman concluded, "He delivered me. He did not forsake me in my hour of need." People stood up, waved their hands in the air, and shouted words of praise to God. After a while, the clapping died down, but then an uproar of thanksgiving would erupt from another corner of the church.

"That is what the hand of God can do!" the pastor said, and this charged the congregation. "He is the I Am that I Am, the unchangeable changer. He has spoken in his word that the sun shall not smite thee by day nor the moon by night."

"Amen!" the hall reverberated. The pastor was silent for a

while and then started cooing into the microphone in his deep dulcet tone: "Amen, and amen, we bless the Lord. Amen and amen." And slowly, quiet was restored for the delivering of the Word.

A male usher in a black suit, white shirt, and red tie hurried to the stage with a fat Bible and a notebook, which he placed on the lectern, performing a slight bow to the pastor before hurrying down the stage.

Back at home after the service, the Utus had jollof rice and chicken for lunch and soft drinks. Bendic asked Paul to tune the JVC to Radio Rivers 2, where Chinemerem Nwoga was presenting her usual Sunday classical music program. Today's edition was about the eighteenth-century pianist Chopin. The presenter played her personal favorites from his work and talked about the pianist's struggle with ill health and the devastating love affairs that might have inspired his music.

Ajie sat on the floor beside the couch. The cold Sprite burned the back of his throat as he gulped. The bottle made a sucking sound, then fizzled and bubbled as he set it down. "I know it was the price for our redemption and all, but if, according to the memory verse quoted in church today, for our sake, it '*pleased* God to *bruise* His own son, Jesus,' does that not then make God a sadist?"

"What did you say?" Ma's eyes narrowed. Bendic was sitting in his chair and didn't lower his newspaper. Ajie's toes played with the velvet buttons on the side of the couch.

"I said, eh, does it make God a sadist then, since it pleased Him to bruise His son?"

Ma's slippers whizzed across the parlor but missed Ajie's head by a wide mark. Ajie sprang up. Ma followed, caught him by the arm, and gave him three clean slaps on the back, *tai!*

tai! tai! They stood there before each other, stunned. Ma could have given more slaps had she wanted: Ajie's feet were glued to the floor like those of an animal dazed before the full beam of a car. He did not know how to run from the hands of his parents. They had never hit any of the children before.

"What's going on?" Ajie could hear only Bendic's voice. He heard Paul open the door to their room and come out. The slaps had carried through the house. Ajie didn't feel any pain—like everyone else, he heard only the sound of the slaps; still his eyes clouded, and the solid edges of the tall room divider became wobbly. He sat down behind the sofa so nobody would see.

"We need to instill the fear of God into these children," Ma strained at the top of her voice. Ajie didn't hear Bendic say anything back.

The next day Bibi dropped one of the dinner plates and stepped right onto a sharp edge that cut through her foot. Later that week, Ma saw Paul with a James Hadley Chase novel and made it clear that she disapproved of the blonde on the cover whose back was turned, showing part of her buttocks, with a holstered gun stuck in her pink lacy panty hose. Paul tried, but Ma closed her face to his explanation that it was just a detective story.

That weekend Bendic called them together and said, "Your mother and I are traveling to America for a few weeks. We don't know if your uncle Gabby will be off work so he can stay with you, but we have spoken to Tam and his wife, and they are happy for you to stay with them while we are away."

ran into a pothole," Uncle Gabby said as he walked into the house, dabbing his forehead with a handkerchief and thumping his boots on the raffia foot mat by the door. "I ran into a pothole near Timber, and my car nearly fell down around me."

The children crowded the door to welcome him. "Just one pothole?" Ma was standing behind the children, smiling and looking Gabby up and down.

"You should have seen the depth of the thing."

"Your car is not made for our roads," Ma replied. "And you are not looking bad at all, Gabby. Money is beginning to touch your hands!" She let her hand drop from his shoulder. "What were you looking for near Timber, anyway?" she continued.

Gabby paused for a moment, frowned, and then said with vague inconsequence, "One girl like that," and Ma thumped his back with her clenched hand, and he ducked a little too late.

"Come and sit down, I beg," Ma said, then moved toward the empty seat right opposite Gabby's. "So you went to see a girl before coming to see us, eh, Gabby? How many months since you last came into town, and a girl—near Timber of all places—matters more?" Ma rumpled her face in mock rancor.

Paul put his hand in Gabby's breast pocket and took out the car keys. "Don't try any rough play," Ma shouted after Paul. "You know you can't drive."

"I know," Paul said. "I just want to check out the inside."

Bibi still held on to Gabby. Paul went to his room to get his bag of mix tapes. He jiggled the car keys at Ajie. To Gabby, he said, "I'm sure your sound system is powerful."

"Paul!" Ma turned to Gabby. "It's like you want them to spoil something in your car."

"Let him go." Gabby laughed. "I'll go out to check what he's doing."

Paul jiggled the keys again at his brother. "Ajie," Paul said with mock impatience, "follow." They hurried out to the driveway, and there was the blip from Gabby's car unlocking. Bibi joined Paul and Ajie in the car but soon heard Ma calling her name, so she went back into the house.

This was a year before the afternoon when everything changed. Before normal life, like a scammer, stooped, touched a finger on the sand, and vanished, and it was hard to imagine it had been there in the first place. The absence of Paul would come to project itself, harsh and relentless, like a whistle at midnight. It would be the question mark hovering above the sentence of their lives, never knowing where to settle.

"So when am I going to see this Timber girl?" Ma asked. "Or is she so ugly that you have to hide her from us?"

"It's nothing serious yet. When I'm off work next, I will come with her," Gabby said.

Outside, Paul and Ajie listened to track after track from the mix tape. They knew every word of Salt-N-Pepa's "Shoop," and they sang and rapped along as it played. "All That She Want" by Ace of Base, coming through Gabby's speakers, made Ajie shut his eyes and sway his head. Paul was sitting nearly sideways in the car with his elbows turned out, as he rapped later to Coolio's "Fantastic Voyage."

Night fell, and they turned on the interior light to read the labels on the cassettes. They reclined the seats as far as they would go when the slow tunes began, and looked like two middle-aged laborers, taking a rest after a full day of carrying blocks on a building site.

"Water Falls" by TLC was playing when Bendic drove in, and they took a break to greet him and take his briefcase and newspapers inside. He asked what they were doing in Gabby's car. They replied, "Nothing," and went back outside to sit in the car.

Bibi came out again to join them. "Gabby can't take time off work, so we are going to stay in Uncle Tam's house for the rest of the holiday," she told the boys.

"Why can't we stay here on our own?" Paul hissed.

CHAPTER FOURTEEN

By Thursday their bags were packed and ready for their two-week stay with Uncle Tam, who lived on the second floor of a two-story building at D-Line. The house was close to a railway track, and near the track was a hub of women who sold roast plantain and fish, corn and pear in their season. There were always people on the streets here, and kiosks were rampant. Some walled compounds had faucets sticking out of block fences where borehole owners sold water to their neighbors.

Ma had given them little lectures on how they should behave. Dishes must be washed right after meals and beds made on waking up. The children were also expected to sweep and keep the house clean. Ma counseled them to ask permission before touching anything and not to oversleep. Bibi would give Auntie Leba a hand in the kitchen, while Paul would supervise the cleaning of the house and the conduct of his younger siblings. "As for you, Ajie," Ma demanded only one thing: "be obedient."

Bendic said he didn't really need to advise the children. They knew what was right and how they ought to behave. However, they were to observe how their hosts did things and try to follow. "Every house has its own culture and pattern of doing things," he said. "When you go there, watch. If there is a table clock that is kept facing east, when you clean the table, don't leave the clock facing west. Pay attention, but enjoy yourselves. Tam and his wife are happy that you are coming."

When Marcus dropped them off on the narrow, tarred street, he waited for the gate to be opened before he drove off.

In all the lectures they received, nobody had bothered to mention that Uncle Tam had a house girl. She now appeared to receive them, since she was the only one at home. As far as Ajie was concerned, such an oversight by his parents was significant. It just confirmed his misgivings about grown-ups, how they constantly missed the point.

The girl held the gate open for them and didn't say a word. Her hair was cut short, like a boy's. She was wearing a long black pleated skirt that was too big for her. She held it up from the wet ground with one hand. She wore white bathroom slippers and no earrings. Ajie was still taking all that in when she said, "I have been waiting for you people since morning. I could have gone to the market and returned by now." She waited for them to file into the compound before closing the pedestrian gate behind them and bolting it shut.

"Is Uncle Tam not at home? Or Auntie Leba?" Paul asked, attempting to take charge of the situation.

"They have gone to work," she replied with a quizzical look, as if Paul should know better than to expect people who worked to be at home at that time of day. "But they told me to wait for you people and show you everything until they return."

The stairs were steep, the banisters rusty and riddled with holes, waiting to drive splinters into any hands running over them.

She walked quickly ahead of them and opened the door that

led to the flat, holding the curtain out of the way. The house smelled of scented soap, and the living room flooring was of plain terrazzo. In front of the set of wooden sofas, a small TV was placed on a sideboard by the wall.

"Uncle said you should relax and feel at home until he returns, and that I should show you your rooms." She looked at Bibi. "Me and you are staying in the same room, so wait." Then to Paul and Ajie, "Two of you, come."

She opened the door to a room and walked right to the center of it. The room was spacious, with high ceilings, filled with the sharp light of afternoon. The curtains were all drawn and tied to a knot. "This is the boys' room," she pronounced with a wide sweep of her hand, as though she were a monarch bequeathing a kingdom to some deserving warriors. Ajie gave Paul a telling look. Bossiness was an instant offender. Paul acted like he hadn't noticed Ajie's face but immediately asked just as she was leaving the room, "So, what is your name?"

She turned around, and a fleeting gentleness crept into her face. "Barisua."

Paul nodded. "My name is Paul."

"I know your names," she responded.

That first night, Uncle Tam made it clear that he didn't mind where they had their dinner.

"I eat in front of the TV all the time," he said. "You are free to join me if you like." So they sat with their plates of rice and stew in their laps, watching a fictional cast of family members scheme against one another on *Checkmate*.

Uncle Tam held a drumstick in his left hand, having rested

his spoon, and tore at the meat with his teeth. His maroon socks were pushed down to a fold near his ankles. He hadn't taken them off when he changed from his work clothes. His blue shorts ran way up his thighs, and just above, there was the heaving mound of his belly and the carpet of hair that continued to his chest.

Auntie Leba was still in the kitchen with Barisua. Because it was their first night, she said, they ought to be given a treat. She had a print wrapper tied over her breasts, and the tiny straps of her chemise showed off her surprisingly slender shoulders and smooth back.

"Dumle was at my office today," she said to Uncle Tam as she came back into the parlor carrying a tray with bowls of fruit salad. "Did I not mention it already?"

"Dumle? What did he want?"

She passed a bowl of the fruit salad to him, and he lapped up some of the juice with a spoon, then put the bowl down on the side stool.

"Dumle can go to hell, as far as I'm concerned. Now that they have seen how powerless we have made them, they are tiptoeing back. What did he say?"

"Nothing, really. He said that he was passing by and stopped to say hello. He said I should extend his greetings to you."

"Indeed." Then he said something in their native Ogoni. Auntie Leba said something back, and Uncle Tam frowned and Auntie Leba laughed.

Dumle used to be a friend of my uncle and auntie," Barisua said to Bibi as they went about cleaning the house the next morning. "Every Sunday after church, he would come here to eat jollof rice and salad. Every Sunday."

Ajie was listening in, waiting to hear what this man had done.

"But now he has become a betrayer." She spoke of him as if he were a family member who had engaged in misconduct and tarnished the family name.

Universities had closed for the semester, but Uncle Tam and Auntie Leba still went out every morning. One day just after they had gone to work and Barisua had done the laundry out on the balcony, she said, "Don't be there thinking that as they go out every day, it's all work they are going to," her voice decidedly casual.

"Okay." Paul nodded.

"They go for secret meetings, too," she said, again in the same tone, as if it weren't a big deal for her to know, although it should definitely be for them. There was an important man from their village, she continued, who had been arrested by the government and kept in detention for over a year now because he had told the government and the oil companies in their village to come and repair the damage they had caused or leave.

Paul's ears flicked. "What was the man's name?"

When Barisua said who it was, Ajie was disappointed. The whole buildup she gave to her story, only to tell them about someone they all knew about. A man who was frequently in the news and whom Bendic and Ma often discussed with their visitors. Bendic had even met him several times in the High Court premises. Barisua flapped a pillowcase, and droplets of water landed on Ajie's cheeks.

"Oh, we know him," Bibi said, but Barisua didn't look like

she had heard and began singing an Ogoni chorus that sounded mournful and celebratory at once.

Ajie took exception to Barisua's attitude, the tone she put up to exclude them, as if she knew things they didn't. Her haughtiness and self-righteousness were barely concealed, the manner with which she went into Uncle Tam's room and came out with a pile of clothes for washing, as if to say she was just the sort of girl whose place in the world it was to carry out such tasks.

When Paul asked her if there was anything they could do, she replied, "Yes. Yes, of course. But nothing really to do for today, maybe tomorrow." Bibi stayed with Barisua and helped her spread out the bedsheets on the line.

Paul and Ajie went to the sitting room, and since there was nothing else to do, Paul turned on the radio, and that was when they heard the news that a plane traveling from Port Harcourt to Lagos had crashed into a forest that morning, minutes before landing.

About an hour after the news was broadcast on the radio, Uncle Tam returned home. He paced the sitting room, asking if they had the phone number of the hotel in Lagos where their parents were supposed to stay before their flight to Boston.

Bibi came out of the bathroom for the third time since hearing the news of the crash. She told Ajie she was having a runny stomach.

"We aren't even sure what flight they went on," Uncle Tam said, looking at Paul.

"No, we are not sure. But we know their flight was for this morning," Paul said.

"Three flights leave Port Harcourt to Lagos every morning, I think."

The doorbell rang, and Uncle Tam went to open it. It was Bendic's friend Dr. Idoniboye.

Ajie looked in the man's face and knew what he had come to tell them: Their parents had been blown into pieces. He could imagine the panic on the flight when the passengers sensed there was serious trouble. Ma would have held Bendic's hand and screamed, "Jesus! Jesus! The blood of Jesus!"

Ajie imagined her clutching on to her faith and Bendic's hand. One of her favorite Scriptures was from the prophet Isaiah: "When the enemy comes against you, like a flood, the spirit of the Lord will raise a standard against him."

She had recently purchased a study Bible that had various commentaries from theologians who argued over the arbitrary commas in the translations of that verse from the ancient Hebrew. Is it the enemy who comes like a flood? Or is it the standard raised by the spirit of the Lord that is likened to a flood? Ma told them, during their morning devotion, that the name of Jesus was the standard that should be raised; the blood of Jesus was equally efficacious. You needed to invoke them in times of trouble. In Ajie's mind during that morning devotion, the blood of Jesus rising like a violent flood cut a more intense picture.

But none of these mattered anymore, he thought as he saw Dr. Idoniboye walk into the flat. Ma's prayers hadn't saved her, regardless of where the commas lay in the sentence.

Dr. Idoniboye said Bendic had called him once he heard about the crash. They knew everyone would be worried about them. "They got on an earlier flight. Just before the one that crashed." He said Bendic had been trying the phone lines in Uncle Tam's department at the university all afternoon but couldn't get through.

"Thank God!" Uncle Tam said, looking at the children. Paul put his hand on his head, gave a big sigh of relief, and sat down on the wooden arm of the sofa. Bibi still looked drained, though her eyes had woken up.

"It's a disaster," Dr. Idoniboye said to Uncle Tam. "Where is your wife?"

"We are expecting her any minute now," Uncle Tam said.

"Your father said I should tell you they are fine," Dr. Idoniboye said again, casting his glance on all three faces. "We are so thankful to God, all of us."

The children left the sitting area, and Ajie could still feel his heart thumping, just as hard as it had when Dr. Idoniboye walked through the door and he thought the worst had happened. Paul opened the door to the balcony and stepped out, and the faint noise of the street filtered in. Ajie and Bibi joined Paul outside, looking down on the street below.

Ajie started feeling ill and went back inside and sat at the dining table. He put his head down on the table, resting his head on his crossed arms. He felt the coolness of the Formica on his arm and then leaned closer to rest his cheek on the table.

"I read that the plane simply exploded in air. Did it have faults before takeoff?" Uncle Tam said to Dr. Idoniboye.

"I don't doubt that it did, but we are hearing all sorts of things," Dr. Idoniboye said, dropping his voice. "That your president wanted some people on that flight dead."

"You don't say."

"Have you not seen the flight manifest? Over twenty solid Rivers men, wasted. Over twenty! Silenced like that in one day. This state has been set back half a century."

Uncle Tam was quiet for a while, and then he asked Dr. Idoniboye if he wanted a drink.

"If it is cold," the doctor said, "I'll take a bottle of malt, please."

When Ajie heard this, despite the burning he was starting to feel on his neck and the recent panic about his parents, he had to smile.

If Bibi had been there, Ajie would have winked at her, and Bibi would have rolled her eyes and shaken her head. Bibi was the expert at mimicking guests. The whole range of them: Bendic's friends, Ma's schoolteachers, Ogibah people, or the visitors who came with trouble tales, seeking assistance.

There was always the guest's initial show of refusal when offered a drink, "No no no! I'm not a stranger now. Don't worry yourself with getting a drink for me."

Ma would cajole. Bendic would say he wouldn't have such nonsense, "You must take something." Then there would be the guest's meek, feeble surrender, mentioning the drink of choice: "Okay, a bottle of Sprite will do."

When the children were younger, they played games like Shopkeeper and Customer, Police and Thief, Guest and Host.

Paul would sit in Bendic's armchair in the parlor with his back straight, his legs crossed like a big shot, with a newspaper on his lap.

"*Kpoi kpoi kpoi!*" A knock on the door.

He wouldn't stand up to open it. He would simply say, "Come in," not even looking up from the newspaper. Then Bibi would sashay in wearing some of Ma's headgear, a stiff jacquard rolled and fashioned into this towering thing that was balanced on her head like a satellite dish. Bibi would move slowly with the double wrapper tied around her waist and the red George wrapper or *asoke* thrown over her shoulder for extra's sake.

Taking off her imaginary sunglasses, she would squint into the room. Paul would get up and stretch his hand in the most restrained and respectable manner; then he would offer her a seat. Pleasantries would be exchanged: How is the family? What about the children? And work?

Bibi wouldn't immediately take the seat that had been offered to her. Like a proper thick madam, she would survey the chair first, adjust the massive falling-down sleeves of her blouse, then finally sit down, resting her big handbag beside her. Then it would be left to Paul, the confident and caring host, to fold away his newspaper and say, "So, madam, what can I offer you?," rubbing his hands together.

They would go through the normal rigmarole of "Oh, no, don't bother." "But you have to take something." She would concede to a bottle of malt. Coke, Fanta, and Sprite were for kids only, or what poor people offered their adult guests.

Paul would raise his voice. "Okon! Where is this boy?"

And Ajie would appear from the kitchen, a houseboy in shorts and singlet, fidgety and ostensibly stupid.

"Yes, Oga," Ajie would reply, falling forward, almost. "Wetin Oga need?"

"Please check on top of the fridge for some cash and buy this lovely lady a cold bottle of malt. Guinness for me, please, and some groundnuts, too."

Bibi would cross her legs this way and then that way, like a businesswoman who had just flown in from Lagos. As they do in television dramas, she would take a deep breath and then ask, "So, sir, how about the contract we discussed over the telephone?"

Here in Uncle Tam's sitting room was Dr. Idoniboye, not going through the ritual of refusal but, rather, accepting and naming his drink of choice once the offer was made: "If it is cold, I'll take a bottle of malt, please."

Barisua set down the bottle and a gleaming tumbler on a side stool. She opened the drink but left the cork sitting on the mouth. "So you are telling me the head of state is responsible?" Uncle Tam asked again, in hushed tones, now that the drink was served.

"That is what we have heard," Dr. Idoniboye replied, in lowered tones, too, as though someone might overhear them. "Some people on the flight had been invited to Lagos for some government function. Only a blind man can't see it."

Auntie Leba returned later that afternoon with a copy of the manifest of the doomed flight, now in circulation.

"Tam!" she called out as she got in. "Tam come and see o!"

They had friends on the flight.

CHAPTER FIFTEEN

The next morning after they finished their chores, Barisua walked across the living room where Paul, Bibi, and Ajie were sitting and turned off the radio.

"What is the meaning of that?" Paul leaped to his feet and turned the radio back on. He surprised himself and the rest of them.

Maybe this morning she only wanted to tease Paul. She would later chide him for his lack of humor, laugh, and turn the radio back on. But now Paul had leapt halfway across the room, shouting, "What is the meaning of that?"

Paul and Barisua were exactly the same height. As they stood staring each other in the eyes, Ajie wondered who was the older of the two. Barisua always acted like she was. She cooked, she cleaned, she went to the market, she woke before everyone else, she followed Auntie Leba's instructions and then laid them down as rules for the three of them. Ajie saw that Bibi wanted to intervene but was holding herself back. From the day they had arrived in that house, Bibi had bound herself to Barisua—faced with her own family of two boys and a fellow girl who was a stranger, she had chosen the girl.

"Paul—" Bibi started, trying to play the mediator.

"Shut up!" Paul shouted at her, looking at Barisua. Barisua walked back to the radio and turned it right off. Paul turned it back on.

"Who do you think you are?" Barisua shouted at Paul. "You little rat. You think this is your father's house?"

"Is it your father's house?" Paul flung back. "Common house girl."

The words seared the air like hot iron. They weakened both Paul and Barisua. Ajie hadn't imagined those would ever be in Paul's vocabulary, but they had come so quickly, so readily, to his lips. Paul hid his shame well, and may have backed down or even apologized, had Barisua not stomped off: "A common house girl, eh?" She went behind the sideboards and unplugged the radio. She pulled out the extension cord and strode off to her room with it. She returned to the parlor after she had hidden the cord and sat down opposite Paul as if to say, *Now what?*

Paul walked into the room he shared with Ajie and shut the door. Bibi and Ajie remained stranded in the sitting room with Barisua.

"Sorry," Bibi said.

"Sorry for what?" Barisua shot back, her voice shaky.

The sky was clear the next morning and a light wind blew steadily through the windows of the living room, lifting the lacy blinds, flapping them sideways. The atmosphere was still tense between the Utus and Barisua.

Paul got up early, washed Uncle Tam's car, swept the parlor, arranged the furniture, puffed the throw pillows, and arranged the headrest cover for the sofas. He took a shower and then sat in the dining area, quietly reading a book. Barisua scrubbed the kitchen floor (asking Bibi several times to stand aside), washed the countertop, brought out the plastic drum for storing drinking water. She scrubbed the bottom of the plastic drum, washed and polished the terrazzo floor, set the kettle to boil for tea, then scrubbed the toilet. At about nine o'clock, the sun heightened and threw a wider light about. The floors, the air, the walls, everything sparkled.

Since Barisua and Paul were not speaking to each other, Bibi and Ajie stayed quiet during breakfast. Paul kept a blank face as he bit into the bread and gulped his warm Bournvita.

At some point Bibi decided to make conversation, asking Paul if he had heard about this or that, turning to Barisua to ask another question. Paul ignored Bibi's small talk, but Barisua responded, her voice loose, easy, and free. She was the type of girl who was always moving, always thinking and taking the road forward. Ajie began to feel a coming headache that began with a dull spreading sensation on his forehead.

Later that evening, Barisua initiated reconciliation. Paul, Ajie, and Bibi were in the sitting room when she stepped out of her room and said, "Bibi, do you want to follow me to the store to buy something?" Bibi sprang up: "Yes." They were all bored, just sitting around the entire afternoon. Then Barisua said, "Paul, won't you come?"

Paul didn't decline.

Paul also didn't decline the next day when Barisua suggested a pillow fight. She knocked Paul hard on the head before he even consented or got ready. He grabbed another pillow and raced after her, and her voice rang out in ripples of laughter.

Although Bibi had never been keen on pillow fights, she didn't want to be left out of the fun this time. She grabbed a pillow and positioned herself, ready to strike. Ajie snatched the last pillow and then jumped on the bed and stood on it. The headache had returned with a pounding on the left part of his head that made him just want to shut his left eye, but he wanted to play, too. Paul went after Barisua and knocked her hard on the side of her head, and she screamed. He lifted the pillow again and brought it down with all his might, right on the center of her head. She fell silent and dropped on the bed, not moving.

"*Ehe!* You have killed her!" Bibi shouted.

"That was my plan." Paul grinned, looking across at the bed where she was lying, playing dead. Bibi bent over Barisua, whose arms were wide apart, eyes closed. "Bari." She shook her by the shoulders. "Bari, Bari." No response. Ajie saw the twitch on Barisua's eyelids and how she held back the smile on her lips.

Paul sat beside Barisua, then shoved his hand under her arms and tickled her. She kicked and gave out a loud yelp, coming out of her pretend unconsciousness. Paul held her down to the bed and tickled her some more. He was sitting on her now, and there were tears in Barisua's eyes, trickling down her cheeks as she laughed. Bibi was laughing, too, looking a bit unsure. Barisua slapped at Paul's hand and kicked her legs as she laughed. Her blue floral dress twisted and ran up her legs. That was when Ajie first saw her panties. They were a very light sky blue, and Ajie was sure he saw a print of tiny pink flowers on them. Ma always got his and Paul's underpants in shades of blue and gray, and Bibi's were always in white, because as Ma said, only dirty girls wore colored panties, but Ajie didn't think this at all—that Barisua was a dirty girl. The soles of her feet were always scrubbed so hard with a stone, each time she came from the bathroom, that they turned a gentle red. She always smelled of Rose talcum powder.

Barisua rolled and wrestled Paul down on the bed. Bibi began to chant, "Bari! Bari! Bari!" Ajie lifted his voice over hers: "Paul! Paul! Paul!"

Bibi clapped her hands in tune to her chants in order to drown out Ajie's voice. Ajie began to bang on the top of a drawer. They did not hear the front door rattle as Auntie Leba let herself in. She had returned home earlier than usual. They didn't see her standing by the bedroom door until she said, "What's going on here?"

They all froze, pillow in hand. Bibi had an unfinished shout in her throat; Paul and Barisua were still entangled on the bed, and as they let go of each other and stood up, Ajie could see their faces change: It was unspeakable joy a moment ago, but it went from self-consciousness to guilt and then shame.

"Welcome, Auntie," Bibi said, and Auntie Leba mouthed a quiet "Thank you" and then gave Barisua a hard look, and it was clear that if not for the houseguests, she would have received a major scolding.

That night they all sat down and watched one of Auntie Leba's favorite Mexican telenovelas. Since they arrived, the children had joined in watching the show, which aired three nights a week. Uncle Tam said it was trash but remained in front of the TV whenever the program started. Barisua sat on a stool by the door where she had a clear view of the screen.

"Stupid man!" Uncle Tam hissed at the TV. "She is deceiving you."

Auntie Leba said, "No, there is a reason why she had to lie to him."

Paul and Ajie still couldn't tell some of the characters apart, and Barisua and Bibi (who caught on early) had to correct them. At some point, everyone was talking back to every scene that came on, sighing, hissing out loud, and lamenting the silliness of the story and of the characters and actors.

"What would you do if it were you?" Bibi asked Paul.

Ajie replied instead, that Leticia never should have forgiven Lothario and let him back in the first place. Auntie Leba had to hurry to the bathroom when the commercial break came on. By the time she came back, the program had returned and everyone volunteered to fill her in on the part she'd missed, including Uncle Tam, whose version of the plot was less accurate than Barisua's and Bibi's.

Ajie still wasn't feeling himself. He had a light fever, his eyes felt dry, and his mouth tasted sour, but he didn't want to bother Auntie Leba, so he kept it to himself. Besides, she might make a big fuss, like Ma did when any of the children got ill, and maybe make him swallow large bitter pills three at a time after every meal. This was much worse than feeling sick.

Before they went to bed that night, Uncle Tam announced that he would be taking them all out to the zoo the following day. "Everyone," he emphasized, which meant Barisua would be going, too.

The storm that came down on Port Harcourt the next morning was unexpected. Ajie was sitting by the window feeling morose, his face up against the cold, damp air coming through the window. He didn't even have to move much to see the roofs of all the bungalows below their building, the NITEL telephone mast, the glass high-rise that had a bank's name on it, and beyond that, in his mind's eye, was the Port Harcourt Zoo, where Uncle Tam and Auntie Leba had taken Paul and Bibi. That morning, he had felt a lot worse and just wanted to stay in bed, so he told Auntie Leba he was feeling tired, that he had a little headache. She began to fuss over him, asking how he was feeling, whether he was running a temperature. Ajie said no, he was just tired, so Auntie Leba told him he could rest at home, and Barisua had to stay back to keep an eye on him. Uncle Tam asked if there was anything he wanted and said they would stop by the shop to get him some goodies.

Now Barisua had turned on the radio, and there was a jingle from the Ministry of Health, a caution against littering that ended with "Keep Port Harcourt clean. The Garden City of Nigeria."

A strong wind lifted and thrashed about the zinc roofs outside, swaying the TV antenna. Barisua stepped in from the balcony and shut the door behind her with a loud bang. Ajie took the book he was reading and headed for the bathroom.

"How are you feeling?" Barisua asked.

"Fine," he said.

"If you are feeling worse, tell me. Uncle Tam gave the instruction that I should look after you," Barisua said, and Ajie just replied "Okay" and went into the bathroom and shut the door.

He didn't feel the need to go, so he sat on the covered toilet bowl with his shorts still on. He turned the page of the book he was reading but wasn't taking in the words. He listened to the sound of the rain on the roof and the wind whipping about outside.

The rain stopped suddenly, and Barisua knocked on the door. "Are you there?"

"Yes."

"What are you doing? Are you giving birth or what?"

Ajie put the book down and frowned at the door. He

imagined her leaning close with her ear by the keyhole, then standing back, arms akimbo, waiting for an explanation when he stepped out.

"I'm just sitting down here," he answered. "I'm just sitting here reading. I don't know what's coming out of me."

"What?" Barisua laughed.

Ajie turned a page of the book.

"You are so funny, this boy," Barisua said, still sounding amused. "You think I have time for you, it's just because you are not well. When you finish, come let's play Whot."

They played three sets of the game and Barisua won all. Ajie shuffled the pack of cards slowly, as if about to deal out, and then hissed and said he was bored and that Whot was a silly game anyway. Could Barisua play Scrabble? He would trash her at that. Was she any good at table tennis? He was the champion now in their house. He trashed Paul most of the time. Bibi, too, except when she cheated, which was often.

"Until we play those other games . . . As for this one, I've beaten you three times."

"I bet it's the only thing you do well."

"You have a sharp tongue! Small boy with bad mouth. If you weren't sick, I would twist it for you until you began to cry."

Ajie laughed. He wanted to tell her he was only joking, but he refrained. He stretched out on the bed and reached for a pillow to rest his head.

"Why do you like making trouble so much?" Barisua asked him.

He had no quick comebacks, and Barisua was waiting for an answer.

"Why do you like making trouble so much?" she asked again.

Most of the questions he had been asked all his life were questions that had previously been asked of other people: questions Paul had grappled with, questions Bibi had supplied answers to, and all he had to do was vary his siblings' response; but right now he was treading water, struggling to stay afloat rather than be drawn in by Barisua's big steady eyes that were on him. He felt that for the first time, another human being was looking at him, really looking at him.

"You always say what you are thinking. I like it."

He pretended he hadn't heard her; he allowed his head to sink deeper into the pillow, and they both fell silent for a while.

Before he touched her, he knew she was not asleep. She was lying there breathing softly, her face turned the other way. He placed his hand on her shoulder like he was about to shake her awake, then he just left his hand there. He let his fingers slide up toward her neck, and Barisua turned around and opened her eyes. Now was the moment for him to say, "I wanted to wake you up," or "Is the paracetamol on the fridge?" But he didn't say any of these things.

Barisua was silent, too. There was the sound of pounding from downstairs, mortar meeting pestle, and voices from the neighbor's kitchen as someone made lunch. The sun was out now, and on the fence outside the window, a red-necked lizard eased himself out of a hole on the wall.

"What are you doing, this boy?" Barisua asked, lying on her side now, facing him fully. She looked bemused but completely unfazed by whatever he might turn up with.

"Nothing," he replied, and hearing his own voice, a familiar thing in this extraordinary landscape, must have been what egged him on. The lines on her neck were a deep brown that could have been purple; he stretched his hand and ran it tenderly over her collarbones. He did not think, *What am I doing?* He was moved by the twin rising of her breasts beneath her cream T-shirt, and her chest that kept breathing up and down. Barisua shifted on the bed and moved closer to Ajie until they were lying with their noses next to each other. She placed her hand on his cheek and pressed her body to his, and ran her hand slowly from the hair on his head to his shoulders, way down to the small of his back. In that moment, all Ajie could think was *So, this is what it means to touch another human being.*

Bendic came to pick them up the next day. The children had been expecting him all morning. Bibi stood on the balcony looking down at the narrow street as cars approached and then went back inside and brought her bag to the parlor. Auntie Leba asked if they had packed all their things and then handed each of them a wrapped gift. "Don't open it yet," she said with a smile. Uncle Tam said he had really enjoyed the children's visit and that he would ask their father to bring them on their next holiday. "Well, I hope they enjoyed their stay," Auntie Leba said jokingly. "We can't force them to come back if they don't want to." Bibi said she had enjoyed her stay, and that besides, they hardly got to visit anyone's house, so this was a rare chance for them. Ajie thought it was weird: Auntie Leba and Uncle Tam asking if they had enjoyed their stay. Couldn't people just tell when someone was having a good time? Why was Bibi giving that speech?

Paul heard the toot of Bendic's horn and shouted, "I think

he has arrived!" and rushed down the stairs. Ajie and Bibi followed, skipping steps and arriving outside breathless just as Bendic was getting out of the car. They ran toward him, and for a moment it wasn't clear if they were all going to run into him in some sort of group embrace, but that was exactly what they did, and the impact of their hug made Bendic stagger backward one step, laughing. "Where is Ma?" "What did you buy for us?" "You are looking so fresh, Bendic." "We were so worried, we thought you were on that plane that crashed."

Uncle Tam, Auntie Leba, and Barisua all came downstairs to join them. The children ran up to get their bags, and when Ajie came down with his, Auntie Leba was talking to Bendic about the plane crash. Uncle Tam mentioned someone the three of them knew who had died in the crash, and Bendic said the husband of one of Ma's colleagues was on the flight. Paul and Bibi came down and put their bags in the trunk. Bendic was telling Uncle Tam about their trip, and at some point Uncle Tam stepped back to look at him, saying, "See how America's cool weather has made your skin so fresh in just two weeks. Sun is killing us here." He shook his head at Bendic in admiration.

Bendic said it was really nice weather for Boston in early September. That it was not too cold, a bit like harmattan weather. Bibi opened the car and invited Barisua to come sit inside with her. Paul got into the passenger seat, straightened out the sun visor to look at the mirror, then closed it up and went to the back to sit with Barisua and Bibi. Auntie Leba looked toward the car, and Barisua kept her face turned toward Bibi so that her gaze wouldn't meet Auntie Leba's—she didn't want anyone to ruin her nice moment with cautionary remarks or maybe sending her off on a errand.

"So you just rushed down to pick up your children

immediately on your return. Do you think something will eat them here if you stay an extra day without seeing them?"

Bendic laughed. "No, they return to school next week, else I would have left them with you for a while." Ajie knew Bendic was only saying things that sounded agreeable without really meaning them, and Uncle Tam was in on the playful exchange.

"And your driver?"

"He resumes tomorrow."

"You are sure you can still drive? When last were you behind a steering wheel?"

"Stop that nonsense," Bendic said with a glint in his eyes. "I drove for over twenty years before I ever needed a driver, and I managed to get here by myself safely, didn't I?"

It was time to go now, so they came out of the car to say their goodbyes. Uncle Tam gave Paul a firm handshake and then drew him close for an embrace. "Goodbye, safe journey, see you soon, thank you, come back again," all were repeated several times, and then they finally got in the car. Barisua hurried to the gate to open it, and Uncle Tam and Auntie Leba followed the car as Bendic reversed and headed out.

Uncle Tam, Auntie Leba, and Barisua stood outside by the gate and waved at the Utus as the blue Peugeot 504 rolled down the street. Bendic honked in acknowledgment. The children waved from the car, and Ajie looked back at the three figures standing and waving by the gate, looking smaller and smaller as their car went farther down the road. Barisua was wearing a brown skirt and a green blouse; she did not stop waving until the Peugeot 504 turned a corner and went out of sight.

On the expressway, Bendic drove slowly in the speed lane. Paul sat in front with him, his eyes on the road. Bibi was squinting outside toward the breeze, her hand gripping the coat hook above the door, looking like she had a mandate to mind that exit. Cars overtook them, and some passengers turned back to give them disgruntled looks. Ajie could see that Bendic didn't care about this. "We have missed you children," he said. Even though Ma was at home waiting, he still said *we.*

This was the moment when Ajie realized that Bendic would one day die. He knew this because real people never said such things to their own children, that they missed them. Only people in films said those things, and everyone knew it was all an act. Film talk. *Love you, Mum! Love you, too. Miss you, Dad! Miss you, son!*

But here was Bendic, saying he missed them.

Whatever was next?

Bendic glanced every now and then in the side and rearview mirrors. His head was still dense with hair but speckled with a rich supply of gray. Looking at him from the backseat, even with the graying hair, Ajie wasn't able to imagine his father as aging, even though Bendic had turned sixty-seven that year.

CHAPTER SIXTEEN

The Port Harcourt International Trade Fair was scheduled for April 4–18, 1995. The jingle was on the radio long before Ajie, Bibi, and Paul returned for their second-term break. The Rivers State Chamber of Commerce, Industry, and Agriculture also sponsored short TV programs to advertise the fair.

The children were in the car heading home after spending the afternoon in Bendic's office. Their car sped under a banner left flapping on a high-tension cable up above the road. *Port Harcourt International Trade Fair. The Garden City welcomes the world.*

They drove past Isaac Boro Park, where sheds, booths, and kiosks had been set up for the fair. Car dealers had erected colorful shops. The TV commercials announced innovative local technology that was relatively cheap but as good as the best the world could offer: portable ovens manufactured in Ilorin, kerosene-run generators fabricated in Awka. Come and see for yourself, the ads implored. There would be sheds for furniture makers and interior designers from home and abroad, displaying standing and decorative wall mirrors, chandeliers, lights, lamps, beds and headboards, boudoir furniture, bathtubs and washstands, chairs, stools, chest drawers, and desks. There would be long rows for textiles, drugs and pharmaceuticals, and engineering goods.

In Shed 33, you would find the renowned trado-medical practitioner, Alahaji Dr. Musa Jubril, whose ads ran most frequently on TV and radio. He had solutions for all ailments stemming from both physical and spiritual sources. He specialized in herbal cures for asthma, barrenness, manhood problems, low sperm count, hypertension, heart disease, diabetes, internal heat, waist, and GBP (general body pain). He would brandish a little wrap of something and say, "This one here, if you put a portion in a bottle and fill with water, *kai-kai,* or any authentic gin and leave it for three days, then drink first thing every morning for one week, it will restore your body, it is also good for cough and for purging your system, cancer cannot come near you, and if you are having bad dreams, too, they will stop."

A long bus painted green and yellow went by the other way and Ajie read out the words written on the side, *Welcome to the Garden City, Host of the International Trade Fair.*

"Why are we called the Garden City?" Bibi asked. There were some trees and flowers about town, Bibi said, but she didn't think they exactly qualified Port Harcourt as a garden.

"Well, it was supposed to be," Bendic began, and then stopped by the lights, where some hawkers shoved their wares into the window.

"Oga, see fresh banana. This na original wristwatch. Buy groundnut, one for five naira, I give you three for ten naira." A boy who was about Ajie's height squeezed some foamy water quickly on the windshield before Bendic could tell him not to bother, then began to wipe it quickly with a brush attached to a long stick. Bendic asked Paul to select some bananas and groundnuts. Eight fingers of banana in a bunch, going for ten naira.

Paul selected three bunches. "Give me these three for twenty."

"Bros, na thirty," the banana seller replied, and Paul made a show of returning them. "Okay," the seller seemed to yield, "take am twenty-five, this na nice fresh banana."

"Twenty," Paul insisted, his eyes now on the red light, a little impatient. "Okay," he conceded, "bring five naira change," and the banana seller braced the tray on his hip and searched his pocket frantically for change before Paul handed him the money. The other boy had finished with the brush and was polishing off the windshield with a cloth just before the lights turned orange, and Bendic gave him some of the change from the banana seller. "God bless you, sir!" He showed a set of white teeth and threw in a salute for Bendic's generous tip as the car sped off.

Bibi was munching already, biting off the banana and throwing groundnuts in her mouth, perhaps already forgetting her question to Bendic about the Garden City.

"The original plan for this town," Bendic began, "was for it to be a small, self-contained space surrounded by gardens and parks." He tried to catch Bibi's face in the rearview mirror. It was named for Viscount Lewis Harcourt, a British Member of Parliament and secretary of state for the colonies, in 1913. Lord Lugard, who was the governor general of the north and south protectorates of Nigeria, wrote to this man, asking if the new port city could be named for him, as no local names were suitable. Lewis Harcourt, however, never visited the city, Bendic said as he turned onto Nzimiro Street, which was at all times shaded by trees and where colonial houses still sat quietly, surrounded by large lawns and short picket fences.

⏳

The person at the gate banged it in a way no sensible person would. Ma stepped out of the kitchen into the parlor, knife in hand, onion tears in her eyes. "Paul, go and check."

It was a Friday, and Ismaila had taken the afternoon off to go to mosque for prayers, after which he would visit his friends who lived near the central mosque at Mile Three.

The visitor, when he was escorted into the living room by Paul, didn't waste time with salutations. "I have come from home," he said.

Ma squinted a little bit. "Are you not Ikpo's son . . . emm, Moses?"

"There is problem," he said, nodding, and Ma became alarmed, dropping the hand that still held the kitchen knife.

"Is your father okay? What has happened?"

"My father is okay." He sounded and looked weak, like someone who had trekked a long distance. "Your husband is not at home?"

As if on cue, Bendic walked into the parlor, tightening the wrapper on his waist. "Soldiers drove into town this morning with trucks. They shot down five boys."

Bendic shouted, "What soldiers? Whom did they shoot?" Ma asked Moses to sit down and made a gesture at Paul to get the tired guest drinking water. Bibi and Ajie were standing near the room dividers as Bendic roared out his questions.

"As we are here," Moses said, "there are people hiding in the bush still. We ran through the bush to Ogbogu. My father said you had to hear at once. The soldiers are still in Ogibah as we are here."

Moses struggled his way through the story. Yesterday, he said, there was an altercation between Ogibah youths and some of the workers on the new gas pipeline construction. The police intervened, but the matter got out of hand when a policeman was hit in the head with a plank. The policeman landed in the hospital, fighting for his life.

The children were all standing in different positions, encircling Moses as he told the story. The smell of something burning was coming from the kitchen, and Ma snapped at Bibi to go turn off the stove, as if it were Bibi's fault.

"Ifenwa!" Bendic was shouting into the phone receiver. "Come, please. Come down at once, are you hearing me?

"Get me my glasses, Paul," Bendic said, and Paul hurried out of the parlor.

When Mr. Ifenwa arrived, they drove out together and Bendic came back very late that night. Paul had gotten the guest room ready for Moses, and Ma asked him if he would like to wash with hot or cold water. "*Ka obula*. Whichever one," he replied.

Bendic left early the next morning. He said he and Marcus would pick up Mr. Ifenwa from his house before they headed out to see if they could get an audience with the commissioner of police. Bendic came back at about ten o'clock that night, and this went on for about two weeks, at which point the soldiers finally left Ogibah. Bendic was among the first people to enter the village after the soldiers left. He went with Marcus and they spent three days there. When they came back, he told Ma her camera battery ran out after the first day and they couldn't find replacements in the shops in nearby villages. He told her he'd heard there had been one or two newspeople who came around, also some organizations, he wasn't sure what they were, but nothing to reflect the scale of the event. "Nothing is left. They brought the whole place down."

Bendic spent that evening looking through the notes he had taken on his tour of Ogibah. Bendic's secretary, Ifiemi, had traveled to her village to see her parents, so the next morning Bendic called Paul into his study and asked him to type out a summary he had made of the event.

"Anything can happen to anyone," Paul said to Ajie and Bibi later that evening, after he was done with Bendic in the study.

It was from Paul that they first heard the details of the killing, how, after gunning down the boys they saw idling away in the square, they burned down Mark Alari's house—the first of many. Old men who couldn't escape into the bush were manhandled and made to lie on the floor. They took, by force, any woman they came across. Houses were defaced with graffiti, and they shat in the town hall. By the evening, when they were done, a great smoke hung over Ogibah, and the air smelled of burning meat as the soldiers rewarded themselves with any livestock they could find, looting Mercury's store and rendering all his cartons of beer empty.

"Anything can happen to anyone. What if they come here to take Bendic and Ma, what will we do?" Paul asked.

But who were *they*? If only Paul could just make that clear. Police, soldiers, or armed robbers? If they came here to take Bendic and Ma, what would you do?

Bibi was silent.

Ajie desperately wanted to supply an answer, but for now he had only questions to ask, so Paul was left to deal with the query all by himself.

CHAPTER SEVENTEEN

Paul spent the rest of the holiday mostly on the veranda, studying for his final exams. Three years earlier, when he was preparing for his junior certificate exams, he had sat on this same veranda before a chalkboard, conjugating irregular French verbs, drawing up Venn diagrams, and locating coordinates on graphs. Paul did not join the other kids who went for holiday lessons in nearby schools. Ma asked a couple of her teacher friends to give him tutorial lessons. Ma and Bendic also read through Paul's textbooks so they could help out with the exercise. Ajie remembered Bendic ticking off some exercises at the end of a chapter on magnetism and commenting with a pencil, "You must work hard."

This time Paul said he didn't want any tutorials from Ma's friends. Ma tried to persuade him—Mr. Daminabo had already agreed to come twice a week for math lessons—but Paul resisted, telling Ma he was fine studying on his own, and Ma clicked her tongue at Paul's rebuff, and Bendic said they should let him be.

It was early evening, and *SuperTed* was on the television, although it was not clear who was watching it. Ajie went out to the veranda and Paul asked, "Have you seen my Ababio?"

Ajie craned his neck into the parlor, leaning backward. "Bibi, Paul wants his Ababio now." Ajie liked this thing of calling textbooks by the author's last name.

"You two should leave his books alone, please," Bendic said. "The young man has an important exam to sit for."

Later, Ma came outside. "It's getting dark," she said, and turned on the light. Paul looked up and returned to his reading. Ma stood for a bit watching him, while Paul pretended he wasn't aware of her gaze. He had become a bit brittle in those final revision weeks, often aloof, always saying he was fine, yes, their parents should just leave him alone for a while. Ajie sometimes felt Ma even wanted to do Paul's reading for him. She brought heaps of past exam questions from as far back as 1985. Bendic seemed to be aware that Paul needed some space but couldn't help himself, either: He would start telling stories about how he prepared for his own finals back in the day, and even Bibi, who enjoyed those stories a lot, would just look at him and want to make him stop.

Ma went back inside the parlor, where Channel 10 was having a break in transmission "due to power failure," Ma hissed, and flipped to Channel 22, where a newsreader was giving the highlights of the evening in Kolokuma language. Bendic looked up when Paul came back into the parlor with his hand full of books. "So when is your first paper?" Bendic asked.

"The eighth. May eighth," Paul replied, dropping his books on the dining table.

"Good. What subject?"

"Chemistry practical." He stretched. "I'm so tired of revising. I want it to come and go quickly."

Paul returned to school one week before Ajie and Bibi. He needed to settle in before his paper, which was due the first week. By early June he had written all nine papers but spent an extra week in school because it was hard for him to say good-bye to his friends and everything he had known for the last six years of his life. He had told Bendic not to send Marcus with the car to fetch him, that he would board a bus and come home on his own, maybe in the company of some of his friends.

He was wearing a pair of blue jeans and a lumberjack shirt with the sleeves rolled up to the elbows when he returned, with a traveling bag slung over his shoulder. He was almost taller than Bendic. Ma said he looked like a university student already, and Bendic agreed.

By August, when Bibi and Ajie were making preparations to return to school for a new session, Paul had bought and completed his JAMB forms, and when Ajie asked him what universities he had picked, he simply replied, "UP and UI." Bendic wanted Paul to go to Ibadan, where he himself had gone. Ma thought staying at a university in Port Harcourt was a better idea, but they worried about the strikes by lecturers. Most universities across the country closed down so often, it was normal for students to spend two to three extra years to complete their courses.

That August, they talked about the student riots, the lack of funding for universities, and how lecturers had to go on strike when their salaries didn't come. They moaned about "this government's complete disregard for education." It was as if the head of state were doing these things to thwart them in particular—he was in direct opposition to Bendic and Ma's happiness. This criminal in an army uniform and sunglasses, he was a complete maniac. He was destroying this country and its future; the only place he deserved to be was in a high-security jail. If you called at 11 Yakubu that August, you would have thought Bendic and Ma were speaking of a very personal enemy.

They talked in low tones sometimes about sending Paul

somewhere abroad to study. "At least we can be sure of the quality of education he is getting."

"But where is the money, eh?"

Ma said Paul was too young to be sent abroad, she wanted him close by. Bendic said he still had friends in England who could act as guardian should the need arise.

CHAPTER EIGHTEEN

Mr. Ifenwa came before dinner that Sunday. He did not come in with his usual dramatic flourish, hailing Bendic's college nicknames, his voice booming from the driveway. He did not come flinging jovial insults and accusations with a newspaper in his hand and an unfinished argument from the last time, wagging a finger at Bendic and saying, "This boy, this boy." He came in under a pile of papers held together in files bound with jute ropes, his face tired, his weak eyes gathering bags beneath them.

"I need to finish marking these papers. I haven't had electricity in over a week, and I'm so busy in the day," he moaned at Ma as soon as he walked into the parlor. He sat down and pushed the files onto the table. When Bendic walked into the parlor, Mr. Ifenwa looked up at him. "At least here is something you can contribute to the common good. I'm hoping if NEPA cuts the power while I'm here, you will turn on your generator so I can finish the work. Let us benefit a little bit from your bourgeois largesse."

"Oh, Ifenwa, be quiet and let me hear something." Bendic laughed and sat down.

"Nne, thank you," Ifenwa said to Ma as the drinks arrived. "I didn't mean you."

"I know." Ma laughed. "Once you put me in that talk, I'll start keeping my cold beer to myself."

He was marking an English exam, and Ma suggested they split the papers between them. They were multiple-choice questions and they could be done in an hour, Ma said. Ifenwa said, "You are a godsend, my sister." He slid some of the papers her way with a copy of the answers.

The telephone rang for Bendic, and he took it in his study and came back a few minutes after. Paul turned up the TV volume and flipped back and forth between the two channels, hoping something interesting would begin on one. Channel 22 was showing a sitcom set in a chaotic house where Chief, his four wives, servants, and innumerable children lived, the sort of house you were never really sure how many people actually slept and ate there. Chief's wives took turns fighting him, and once, when he'd annoyed everyone, all his wives and children came together to beat him up. He looked ridiculous, threatening them afterward, pointing and huffing. Ajie thought the program stupid and not funny at all.

"The roadblocks are worse today," Mr. Ifenwa said, placing a marked script on the increasing pile to his left. He and Bendic began to talk wistfully about the kind of student protest they had in their day, their student union governments, and what they were able to accomplish. "What would you do"—Mr. Ifenwa turned his gaze on Ajie—"if you were the president of this country?"

Ajie laughed.

"Yes, tell me," Mr. Ifenwa said, his eyes still on him. Then he looked at Bibi and at Paul in a way that made it obvious the question would be coming to them, too. Ajie didn't know

198 | JOWHOR ILE

what to say first. He wanted constant power supply, but saying that would make him sound self-serving. Okay, he would
give jobs to the jobless; he would try to make poor people
not poor, and to pay lecturers so they wouldn't go on strikes
anymore. He definitely wouldn't send a letter bomb to kill
any journalist who wrote things about him he didn't like.
He would not make people disappear, as the current head of
state was known to do. But he didn't say any of these to Mr.
Ifenwa.

"I'd make sure the roads were well maintained so they didn't
cause accidents," Ajie blurted, and regretted the words immediately because he'd just remembered that Mr. Ifenwa's wife had
died in a car accident.

The parlor went quiet. Ma's hand floated midair with the
paper she was about to put aside; Mr. Ifenwa blinked behind
his oval lenses, and Bendic cleared his throat, and the air in the
parlor lurched back into gear.

"I'd send the military back to the barracks and return the
country to democratic rule," Bibi said.

Bendic hummed as if unsatisfied with the answer. Ma circled
a number for Mr. Ifenwa's attention and then passed the paper
to him. "I would sack all the ministers and military administra-
tors. They are all corrupt," Paul said.

"Just that?" Bendic asked.

"And throw them in jail."

"Without a fair trial first?" Bendic asked. "Sounds authori-
tarian."

"Sounds like the kind of revolution we need, if you ask me,"
Mr. Ifenwa said without looking up from his work. "How much
evidence do we need that our leaders are corrupt?"

"I mean," Bendic continued, "the problem is obviously systemic, and resolving it will require more than the actions of one good man or removing people from positions. It's about developing processes, checks and balances, and organizing ourselves in a good way."

Mr. Ifenwa's nostrils flared and he gave out a sigh of frustration. "It makes me a little crazy when you keep saying *systems*. You have that maniac in power, murdering ordinary citizens, people are disappearing every day. Someone should first make him disappear, and then we can talk of moving this country forward!"

Bibi was bristling on her seat; Bendic and Mr. Ifenwa had hijacked the conversation instead of letting her expound on how she would make Nigeria better, so she began to flip the channels but kept the volume low. Ma asked Paul to bring her handbag from her bedroom.

When Paul came back to the parlor, Ma had brought up the case of the mysterious disappearance of a journalist who was a colleague's relative, and Bendic said that perhaps it was high time everyone took to the streets, or else they ran the risk of being plucked off in isolation one by one.

Bendic and Mr. Ifenwa talked into the night, long after Ma had done most of the marking and teased that Mr. Ifenwa had just brought the work for her while he spent the time arguing with Bendic. Bibi had fallen asleep on the couch, and Ma shook her gently and asked her to go to bed. She sat up quickly with her back straight and said she wasn't sleeping. Paul was sitting beside her. His eyes were on Bendic saying something about "street politics."

They stood up to escort Mr. Ifenwa to the gate, except for

Bibi, who had fallen asleep again. Mr. Ifenwa kept saying, "Nne, thank you," to Ma, and said he should hurry home now, as it was late. "Friday," he said.

"We are here," Bendic replied.

After they had said good night and Mr. Ifenwa had walked down the road, Ismaila came and locked the gate for the night with a heavy iron chain and a big padlock.

ibi saw the crowd first and then leaned out of the car to get a better look. A slow line of traffic was building up in the other lane. Ma didn't tell Bibi to get back into the car and not waste the coolness from the air conditioner. She was way too tired from all the haggling and trekking about the market and was in no mood for talk, so she switched off the air conditioner so they could all feel the heat, and maybe Bibi would behave herself and shut that window.

Bibi was still looking outside. "It's like the riot is happening in front," she said, and Ajie put his head out the window to get a look. "I won't be surprised," Ma responded, looking up as the lights turned orange. "Let us pick up your skirt and get home, then they can riot all they like." The family had just left Mile One Market after half a day of trudging stalls and bargaining for school supplies. "I hope you are both settled for school now. Anything you haven't mentioned will have to wait till when you come home on your midterm break. No more buying. I think we've done just enough."

The students swamped the lane as they marched so that cars couldn't go through. Some had placards held up high with sticks, while others pinned them on their bodies. Hawkers solicited from the sidelines with trays of mangoes, baskets of oranges, and soft drinks. A small group of students gathered around a hawker who had set down his basin for the students to take water tied up in clear freezer bags about the size of a big fist. The line of cars held up by the protesters stretched the entire length of Aggrey Road. A young man jogged ahead of the crowd. He waved his hands like a traffic warden and shouted something to those nearest to him. Then they all started moving to the right and formed a dense pack on one side of the road, giving way for the traffic to flow.

"It's a peaceful demonstration," Ma said to Bibi, "not a riot."

"I hope they burn some government cars," Ajie said.

Ma turned her head to face him. "What do you mean by that?"

"They should burn some government cars, destroy a few things, then they'll get some attention."

"Have you seen the mobile police waiting to pounce?" Bibi offered.

"Let him sit there and talk nonsense."

"It's not nonsense. If my school were in town, I would join."

"You will not join in anything like that."

"They are university students, anyway. Can you see your age mates there?" Bibi said.

"Paul is entering university soon."

"You are not Paul."

"Doesn't matter. If he joins, I can follow."

"Yaya yaya ya, talk talk talk."

"Quiet, the two of you!" Ma shouted. "Let me hear something, please."

Green leaves were stuck onto car fenders to show solidarity with the students. Some drivers shouted support from their windows. A bus driver held out a clenched fist. His bus had not just green leaves but a young tree branch. It tilted forward each time the bus slowed, as if bowing down to the road. A loud Oliver De Coque tune blared from his windows as he drove past, leaving behind an air of jubilation.

They got to Borokiri, and it was time for Ma to wonder aloud if the tailor had finished making Bibi's skirt. Twice she had failed to have the skirt ready on the agreed date. With only a few days remaining before their return to school, Bibi's wrap-around sport skirt was the only item left to tick off on their list.

"What is it with tailors?" Ma parked the car a block away from the shop. "Bibi, pass me my handbag." She opened the door and climbed out of the car.

They walked down the block and crossed the concrete slab over the smelly gutter and stepped into the tailor's shop. A young woman was working the sewing machine with her hands and feet. "Welcome, madam." She stopped pedaling when she saw them. "My madam no dey, but she keep something for you," then she went into a back room.

Several almanacs of women dressed in different styles were hanging on the wall. One almanac was captioned *First Ladies' Designs*. A model was pictured in all the shots, sampling Ankara fabrics. Ma took a seat as they waited, and Ajie wondered if the model sampling all the different Ankara designs had taken all those pictures in one day.

Ma stood by the curtain while Bibi tried on the skirt. Ma kept asking, "How does it feel? Is it tight? Is it comfortable? It's sportswear. You should feel free and relaxed in it," Ma went on, even after Bibi had indicated it fit her well and that she was comfortable.

The next morning, Bendic and Ma left early for work. The rain came down heavily from dawn till about midday. When

NEPA restored power, Ajie went to the parlor and turned on the radio. As he lay on the sofa, his mind was filled with the mix of fear and excitement that he had always associated with returning to school. He made a mental list of the things he needed back in school, legal and contraband. He thought of how school life might change for him now that Paul wasn't there. Ajie could hear Bibi talking to Paul in the corridor and Paul was saying, "I have no idea where it is." He heard Bibi go into the bathroom, and after a while came the whirring sound of Ma's hair dryer.

Paul was standing, leaning on the room divider in the parlor, on this Tuesday morning when rain had left all of Port Harcourt soaked and dripping. He bent a little to tune the big radio—he turned the knob slowly, deliberately, so that there was the voice and static and voice again, as happens when one tunes a radio. And this irritated Ajie as he lay there on the couch. He heard the hair dryer go on for a long time and then fall silent for a while.

It was only eleven-forty-five a.m., because on Radio Rivers II the *News in Special English* had just begun: "Country-people," the newscaster said, "na the things wey dey happen for this country I want tell una so." The voice was low and familiar. "Him name na Boma Erekosima."

Here was Paul, in shorts and singlet and a Carl Lewis haircut that needed shaping up, on the day when he would eventually disappear.

CHAPTER TWENTY

E veryone forgot Bibi was supposed to return to school that Saturday, until Marcus, with his sense of duty, whispered it to Ma right after Bendic had returned from the TV stations to schedule an announcement that Paul was missing. Marcus said, "Madam, your daughter go still go today?"

Ma just stared at him and did not know what to say. Her eyes were glassy wet. She glanced at Bibi, who was standing about, not knowing what to do with herself or how to be. "I am sorry, Bibi," Ma mumbled.

Bibi could have said something back, like she didn't really need to go that day; that it was fine, there were other things. Paul was still missing after four days. But she just nodded.

Before Bendic went to the radio and TV stations, Ma had to find a picture. "A recent picture," the office manager at the TV station had said to Bendic over the phone when he called to ask what was needed. Ma went through the photos and couldn't decide which to choose. She pulled out a photo album with a heavy brown cover and spiral binding; she flipped through the pages, looking for something that might be suitable.

This was the album she didn't like the children playing with. It had all the important pictures taken from when the children were only babies, in napkins and napkin pants. None of them had any tops on in their baby pictures, just talcum powder rubbed all over their necks and chests. Bibi was crying in hers.

Paul was leaping up to catch something, and Ajie had a steady glare, his dark eyes holding the same expression then that they always would: accusation, gripe, and the dancing impulse to pick up something and throw it.

There was the picture to mark Paul's one-year anniversary, and another where Paul was receiving a prize for being the best student in his year. And there was Paul in his school uniform when he first entered secondary school. There was a studio photo Paul had taken only a few weeks before. By himself, he had gone to Majestic Photos, a new studio that had opened on Sangana Street and was quite the talk of town. He was wearing dark green denim trousers and a big T-shirt. He had a fresh haircut. The photographer, it seemed, had encouraged him to powder his face before the shot. He was resting his hand on a high stool, and his foot was stepping on the base as he stared into the camera. That was the picture Ma pulled out of the album and handed over to Bendic. Bendic murmured some words and left the house. Ajie heard the car start and Ismaila disturbing the gate.

That evening, the announcements came up for the first time; they had told Bendic when the announcements would be aired. Ma looked at the television and then stood up and walked into the kitchen once Paul's picture came on the TV screen. The background noise in the studio and how Paul's picture shifted slightly on the screen every now and then made it feel exactly like the obituary announcements that came on Friday evenings.

The announcer began to say that a boy aged seventeen had gone missing. Then Ajie heard a sound from the kitchen like an animal being strangled. Bendic went into the kitchen to meet Ma, and Ajie could see Bibi staring at the TV, but he didn't want to look at it anymore. Above the TV was a calendar that, for the month of September, showed some *Atilogwu* dancers enraptured in the ecstasy of the music, grinning wildly in their raffia skirts.

Bendic stayed with Ma in the kitchen for a while. When they came back to the parlor, Ma's eyes were red and puffy.

On the day Bibi was actually to return to school, Ma woke her up early. Ajie was still in his room while Ma went through Bibi's tin box to see if she had all she needed. He didn't hear them talk. Ma had said she was going to drop Bibi at school. When Ajie came out to the parlor, Bendic was standing by the window, looking into Ma's garden, and did not realize he wasn't alone until Ajie greeted and startled him. He turned around, and Ajie was not sure what it was he saw on Bendic's face— fright, surprise, wonder, or anguish?

"Oh, it's you?" Bendic said, trying to regain his composure. "I hope you don't mind, we will take you back to school tomorrow. Is that okay? I rang Mr. Onabanjo this morning. I left a message for him, explaining that there were some problems, but you'll be in school tomorrow. Okay?" He did not say, *So be a good boy, be a big boy, be strong, your brother—we will find him*. He turned his face back to Ma's garden.

Bibi appeared in the doorway from the corridor. Her hair was neatly done in cornrows, and Ajie wondered if Ma had done it herself this time. They hadn't had the time to take Bibi to the woman in Mile One Market who normally plaited her hair. Bibi was now a senior student, so she was allowed to wear a skirt and blouse instead of a sleeveless pinafore and blouse.

Ma's feet hurried out of the kitchen. "Where is my car key? I kept it on the fridge. Has anyone seen my car key?"

Bendic looked on top of the TV near him. "Have you checked on top of the fridge?"

Bibi wheeled her box to the side of the room divider. She went back into the room and got two other bags and then stood there. "Let us go, Bibi," Ma said, and the keys jiggled as she walked to the door.

Bibi just stood there. "Oh," Bendic said, "let's help her with the box. It is heavy, Ajie, come give us a hand, please."

Ajie took one of the smaller bags and then bent to lift the trunk, with Bendic on the other side. Bibi's sharp cry cut through the room before she fell to the ground. It was so quick, how she dropped onto the parlor floor. "I don't want to go anywhere," she sobbed. "Where is Paul? What has happened to him? I don't want to go anywhere. Don't make me go."

"Edobibi, Edobibi." Ma ran to her. Bendic looked like he had been struck. He wanted to rush toward Bibi, he wanted to say something to her, but the words got stuck in his throat. He stepped forward and swayed and held on to the sideboard like an old man leaning against a stick.

Ma sat on the floor beside Bibi with her legs fully stretched out. Then she straddled Bibi, holding her close to her chest. Ma loosened her wrapper a bit and used the edge to wipe Bibi's tears. "I kwa ye. Don't weep."

Ma dropped Bibi off at school later that morning.

The next day Marcus took Ajie to school. When anyone asked him how Paul was, he told them Paul was fine, but then word soon spread from students who lived in Port Harcourt that Ajie's brother was missing and there had been announcements on the radio and television.

CHAPTER TWENTY-ONE

I t is a Friday in November 1995, and schools have shut down for midterm break. Bendic and Ajie are huddled over the JVC radio in the parlor as Ajie tries to tune the dial on the side for clear reception. Bibi is out with Ma and Auntie Julie. Auntie Julie and Ma have been on a tour of many churches for some time, seeking answers and not quite finding them. Ma had told Ajie and Bibi when they came home for the break that she had just returned from Benue state, in a place where a Catholic reverend father was famed for praying down solutions to problems; it was said he had a special audience with the Virgin Mary, whom many seekers to this prayer ground had testified to seeing in an apparition.

Ajie did not know how Ma, who once looked down on Catholics for what she called their idolatry, who had always been uneasy about rituals with incense, beads, holy water, and figurines, could actually have followed Auntie Julie to a Catholic prayer ground. When Ma told them of her trip, there was a wild blaze in her eyes, and Ajie could tell that she would have gone anywhere if an answer to her request were promised. She would have gone to an imam, a native doctor, an Indian shaman, a marabou in Cotonou, even.

"You don't know whom God can use," she had said to them. "God can use anybody He wants, He has the power. He has used a donkey before, made a donkey speak to a man. It is His world, and there is nothing He can't do."

Ajie would have loved to tell her, just following from her logic, that if God can do anything, then he should just bring back Paul in an instant, in the same quick way in which he disappeared. But he couldn't say that. His mother was disappearing, too, right before him. Ma hadn't done her hair in months; he could see the thick undergrowth graying where her scarf went askew on her head.

Auntie Julie arrived early that morning, and soon after, she and Ma and Bibi drove out in the car to meet a woman of God whom Auntie Julie referred to simply as "Mummy."

"The woman pack anointing," Auntie Julie assured Ma. This woman of God could only speak in Igbo, so before they left home that morning, Auntie Julie told Ma she should write her prayer request on a piece of paper. Bibi wrote hers, too, even Auntie Julie did, and Ajie was sure they had all written the same thing and were somehow hoping that if answers were being rationed, at least they stood a greater chance of being granted their single request.

That past September, the house had been full of visitors and sympathizers, people offering help, saying, *No, it can't be, there must be something we can do.* By October the number of visitors had trickled down. Mr. Ifenwa still came around as often as before, but he and Bendic would sit in the parlor, and you wouldn't hear them talk or laugh like before. Paul's friend Fola came around every day. In the early days after Paul disappeared, he told Ajie not to worry; he patted his shoulder, "He's going to come back." There was even a sense of excitement in Fola's voice as he said this to Ajie, as though this were one of those mystery stories they read where, finally, at the close of the book, the mystery is solved and all the loose ends tied up in the most satisfying ways. With nothing else to talk about apart from Paul's disappearance, Fola dropped in less and less.

When misfortune befalls you, people secretly blame you. Ajie noticed this. People can't help it. They do it so they can believe it won't happen to them. They haven't done whatever it is you have done to deserve such suffering. They see you on the street and look away, and if they can't avoid meeting you, they talk about other things. It's as if you are a tainted thing, someone who could possibly bring bad luck.

A few weeks after Paul went missing, the story eventually went stale among their neighbors. Fola passed his SAT and got a place at a university in Oklahoma. Before he left, he came over to see Ajie. He showed him the university brochure, which featured pictures of students sitting outside on the lawn, dressed in jeans and T-shirts, laughing, drinking juice, looking in books. He said he would write to Ajie once he got to Oklahoma.

On this Friday morning, Ajie and Bendic are huddled over the JVC radio in the parlor. BBC World Service isn't clear enough. "Try Voice of America," Bendic suggests.

The nine Ogoni activists who were detained for over a year by the military government were recently tried, and a few days prior, the Provisional Ruling Council announced it had approved their execution. The news sent everyone reeling. It wasn't possible; that wasn't even a trial. Earlier that day Ajie overheard Bendic saying to Ma that there was no way the activists were going to be executed. "The international community will whisk them out!" Ajie imagined a secret operation led by some foreign commandos stealing into the prison cells and evacuating the activists, just as it happened in films. One of the men was an outspoken author and playwright who had denounced the government and the activities of the oil companies that had brought environmental damage to his community and impoverished his people. Uncle Tam knew this man well and had been to many meetings and rallies with him. The day of the scheduled execution, right after Ma, Bibi, and Auntie Julie left to see the woman of God, Bendic asked Ajie to tune in to a foreign radio station, since no local news could be reliable.

It is unusually warm in the parlor. Bendic has a wrapper around his waist; he has pulled up a seat next to the divider where the radio is. He mutters that the military dictator might be crazy, but he wouldn't do this. They get clear reception.

It is a man's voice coming from VOA, confirming that the men were found guilty, and all nine of them were hanged earlier that morning.

"Animal!" Bendic shouts. "Animal! Animal!" he shouts over and over again. He and Ajie are still sitting beside the radio as comments flow in from studio guests. After a while Bendic stands up, gathers his wrapper a little tighter around his waist, and then shuffles to his bedroom.

Ajie returned to school the next week. One Tuesday afternoon during a boring business studies lesson, he saw his guardian standing by the class door with Ma by his side. They went with Ajie to his dormitory to get his things.

Mr. Onabanjo told Ma he would speak with Ajie's form teacher to see if his test results could be used to assess him for the term; school was shutting down for Christmas break in two weeks anyway, so he would not be missing much.

Ma didn't say much to Ajie throughout their journey back to Port Harcourt. Ajie did not ask her any questions, either.

He didn't think they had found Paul. He was too afraid to ask if anything had happened to Bibi. He thought maybe something worse had happened in Ogibah, or maybe 11 Yakubu had burned down and they had nowhere to live.

Nothing at all made him think to ask anything about Bendic.

IV

CHAPTER TWENTY-TWO

Finally, it is evening. The lights come on in the new high-rise shop that was built across the street, and Ajie sees that there are men sitting, drinking beer, on one of the balconies. Their loud voices and laughter reach him, and he stands up to push the window out a little. Ismaila is outside the gate, talking to a man. Ajie heard the gate rattle and thought it was Ma returning from church. He steps out and sees it isn't Ma. It is a man dressed in a faded blue *babariga. Maybe the neighbor's gateman,* Ajie thinks.

He returns inside. There is something strange about standing in the room you grew up in after you have been away from home for a very long time. To look at the bed you slept in when you were eight or thirteen and still are expected to sleep in at twenty-six.

Paul's bed is still there by the window, and the reading table is still wooden and brown, with all the old nicks, scratches, ink-blots, and dull gleams of candle wax.

Outside the window, the air darkens, and Ajie hears Ismaila laughing.

He steps outside and tells Ismaila he is going for a stroll. "No problem," Ismaila says, "I go tell madam when she return from church."

Ajie turns left at the lights, veering from Nzimiro. There are many more bikes on the roads than there used to be. Even in this once reserved part of town, there is a disproportionate increase. Light, handy, and fast, these bikes have a mild insouciance about them. Something playful and bad-tempered at the same time. Yesterday, stuck in traffic for about an hour on the way from the airport, Ajie left the driver in the car and hailed a bike. He hadn't returned to Port Harcourt after five years, he said to himself, only to be trapped in the hot stickiness of a small car held up on East-West Road. He took a seat on the well-padded pillion, and when the Okada man moved the bike, he felt the rush of wind on his face, inside his shirt, and on the back of his neck. He could see Port Harcourt again, but not through a car window.

He approaches the barbershop on Ogoja Street. It seems wider than he remembers it, and full of light. He can see the mirrors, and the little generator outside trembling and puffing smoke. A boy, nearly as tall as the door, pushes the lacy blinds to one side and walks out. He pauses midstep, pats his hands over his pockets, front and back. Keys, wallet, mobile phone, what has he forgotten? He turns around and steps back into the shop.

There have been times when Ajie would turn a street corner or look into a car and see someone's back, a profile or head that looked just like Paul's. He understands how these things work—it's just his mind playing tricks on him. Still, he would increase his pace, and when he got close enough to the stranger, he would stare a little bit too long.

Once, on the London Tube, he sat opposite a boy wearing dark green skinny jeans. There was a quality to this boy's nose, his eyebrows, his boots, the way he stood up when the train stopped at Moorgate station. There was a something Paul-like about him. Ajie saw it right after the boy sat down opposite him, so he placed his eyes on him and kept them there. Their eyes met. The boy looked away, but Ajie didn't. The train wobbled in the track and howled, and then the boy returned the stare, attempting some kind of feeble protest: *What are you looking at?* he seemed to ask. When the boy stood up to leave the train at Moorgate, he picked up his backpack from the ground, and Ajie saw it was the same army-green as Paul's bag, the one he carried on that day he left the house over a decade ago, on another continent. Ajie stood up a little too late to follow the boy, and the doors beeped and slammed shut in his face.

On Herbert Macaulay Road, he wants to point out to Paul that the video club has been demolished. He wonders aloud in disgust at why so many shops have been built so close to the road.

There is a huge billboard advertising a mobile phone network, a young man and woman holding phones to their ears and smiling lovingly at each other. Just beyond that is a billboard advertising a church. The pastor, a man in a shiny suit, is smiling with his hands held together on his chest; his wife, a woman in a red skirt suit and a large black hat, is to his right. Farther down the road, there are more billboards, posters stuck on fences, on electric poles and transformers, of preachers with a variety of titles—bishops, apostles, prophets, evangelists, pastors, and reverend pastors—inviting members of the public to different church programs: Night of Encounter, Operation Claim Your Victory, At the Red Sea: Your Enemies Must Drown. They promise a "power-packed" event where the Word would be shared and miracles will manifest. Some note that they will be "ministering, in partnership with the Holy Ghost."

They all promise divine favor, fruit of the womb, increases in business, prosperity, healing, open doors, and freedom from demonic oppression.

A white Jeep pulls up right beside him, and Ajie stops walking. A woman in a blond weave sticks her face out the window to ask if he knows the way to Atako Street. He points in the direction of the street, which is in fact the very next turn. After she drives off, he notices a small banner tied to a transformer, fluttering a little in the breeze, and on it a minister with the title "Field Marshal of the Most High," inviting the public to a night of answered prayers specifically tagged: Lord Give Me a Spouse Lest I Die.

Ajie follows the road heading back to Nzimiro and wonders about Mrs. Braide, their former neighbor from number 6. She used to go to a church like these. When they were children, Ma and most people they knew viewed those places of worship with suspicion. Now, he thinks, there is such a mania for them. When did this change?

Ma said Mrs. Braide had relocated to Abuja after kidnapping got rife in Port Harcourt in the past couple of years. Armed militants who claimed they were struggling to get a fairer deal for the oil-producing minorities who had been neglected by government began kidnapping European oil workers for ransom.

These days, since the number of European workers has dwindled, just about anyone is up for grabs if you are deemed wealthy enough to cough up some money, or your family or friends are. Local criminals have found a new trade.

Ma told Ajie that sometimes the negotiations for ransom scaled down from millions of naira to hundreds of thousands, then down to tens of thousands, when it became obvious the captive's family really had no money. A band of kidnappers begged a family to send them mobile phone credit, at least, to cover the captive's call cost and feeding expenses for the two weeks. Sometimes kidnappers just ceased making contact with the captive's family even when negotiations were going well, and they would later learn or simply accept after waiting for months that their loved one had died from an illness or been shot by accident. Ma warned Ajie to be careful, not to let people know he had come from abroad, since they might think he was rich, and Ajie just looked at her and wondered how he could be kidnapped from his own streets.

As he turns onto Yakubu Avenue, Ajie spots Ismaila and his friend from a distance. They are now two little black things crouched on their haunches, like professional beggars at Garrison Junction. *Are they writing on the sand or what?* he wonders.

"Madam done return," Ismaila says to him.

"Oh. Okay. Thank you, Ismaila."

Ma is in the kitchen, standing over the sink. "You did not eat your food." She wipes her hand on a kitchen towel and hangs it back on the peg. She uncovers a ceramic bowl on the gas burner, then puts it back. There is boiled yam in it.

"I will eat later."

Ma opens the fridge and takes out a bottle of Sprite and hands it to Ajie. "It's Sprite you like, *abi*?" Then, "Oh, sorry, it might ruin your appetite. Except you want it." She lets him decide, and Ajie says thanks, that he will have the Sprite with his meal.

"Has Bibi confirmed when she's arriving?"

"Tomorrow." Ma runs her hand over the top of the fridge for an opener. "First flight."

"With her boyfriend?"

"Her fiancé."

"Boyfriend," Ajie says. "She hasn't said she wants to marry him."

"Fiancé," Ma says firmly, her mouth about to smile.

Ajie is in her way so that she brushes against him as she passes. He goes into the garden and is confronted with Ma's expanded taste in plants.

CHAPTER TWENTY-THREE

Throughout Ajie's ten-year sojourn abroad, Ma was always a morning caller. Nigeria and Britain were in the same time zone for most of the year, yet each time Ma called, he felt a lapse he could never explain or shake off, like she was speaking from the past, a gaping void with muted echoes.

After he finished boarding school, he left Port Harcourt for St. Albans, an English city which at first felt to him more like a medieval town, with its stone wall, church bells, and oak doors that give onto the narrow cobbled streets. He attended sixth form there and lived as a boarder in the house of a middle-aged widow, Mrs. Heath. Ma would call on the landline by eight in the morning. "Why are you still in bed? I can hear it in your voice. Don't you have class today?"

He left Hertfordshire, moved to London to study electrical and electronic engineering at Imperial College, and then began to do the Friday-night pub crawls that left him groggy and hungover until two P.M. the next day. He started missing Ma's calls. *Sorry. Call you back in the evening,* he would text her. He wouldn't return her call, and Ma would ring him again on Sunday morning before heading to church.

Why does she never call in the afternoon or when I'm not in bed?

Throughout his years at university, during his one-year

internship, and when he began his first proper job working for a digital media company at Kings Cross, Ma would always ring him twice a week: once on the weekend, and again in the middle of the week.

Last week his phone rang, and Ma's voice came through: "Where are you?"

"I'm at home," he replied. He almost joked, "Standing in the kitchenette of my flat in the North London borough of Camden, and where are you?" But something in Ma's voice stopped him. "I'm at home. Are you okay, Ma?"

"I need you to buy a ticket as soon as you can."

"A ticket."

"Yes, if possible for tomorrow—you can tell them at work that it's important. A man has just left here, says he's a pastor. It's about your brother, Paul. Can you get a ticket? I have sent for your sister, too."

CHAPTER TWENTY-FOUR

I t is not enough to confess your sins and receive forgiveness from God," the man sitting before Ma began. "Even though the blood of Jesus washes your slate of sins clean, you have to go back to the people you've wronged in the past and try to make things right. Some Christians these days believe this is some obsolete Old Testament doctrine, but it's not. A true believer must make restitutions for his or her wrongs. The Bible shows us ways of doing this; this is not about trying to pay people off, no. If, for instance, you steal something from someone and you one day repent of your sins and God forgives you, shouldn't you go to the person you stole from, apologize, and then give back what you have stolen?"

Ma waited to see where it was all going. She had been in her back garden, weeding, when Ismaila called out to say she had a visitor. It could have been anyone, relatives always dropped by. Perhaps it was someone from Ogibah who would want to spend the night, or one of Bendic's former colleagues. Once someone had come in to inquire if she was looking to sell the house, and Ma didn't know how to respond, so she just said no, as if it weren't such an unusual question to ask in the first place.

Ma came inside through the back door and let the man in. He was dressed in a black suit, red shirt, and black tie. There was something captivating about the way he went about what he had to say. Every word seemed completely needful, every sentence; the way he enunciated some words, gesturing with his hands in order to illuminate them; it was as if the turning of the world depended on the things coming out of his mouth.

"I used to be a mopol," he continued. "For six years, I did mobile police work. Between 1994 and 1995, they stationed me in Port Harcourt. I want you to take what I'm going to say calmly. God sent me here to come and make peace, because I saw something, and I think it's only right that you should know about it."

Ma, looking a little alarmed: "What is this about?"

The pastor hesitated, inched closer to the edge of the sofa, and linked his fingers together. "During the student riots that year, '95 to be exact, an accident happened with a boy. He was not among those rioting, but one of my colleagues stopped to search him. It was just the work of the devil."

"What are you saying?" Ma shot to her feet. "What are you saying?" Ismaila, who had been eavesdropping in the veranda, was now standing by the parlor door. Ma picked up the vase on the center table and hurled it at the pastor. "My son! My son!" She grabbed the man by his black tie and slapped him all over the head and shoulders. "My son! My son!" she kept shouting as Ismaila rushed to her side, trying to restrain her. "Madam, wetin him say happen?" Ismaila turned around to shout questions at the pastor, but the pastor just held his hands together in a quiet demeanor, his face placid, his eyes gentle like a dove's.

The student demonstration had been peaceful all morning. It was raining, and most of them had gotten drenched in the downpour. At about midday, the sun came out and warmed up their enthusiasm. More students arrived. The mobile police, who were there to keep a close watch on the demonstration, had received strict instructions to keep things under control at all cost. Word circulated that another group of students had burned two government cars near Eastern Bypass.

Some students began to hurl stones in the direction of the police. The police shot some tear gas canisters and some bullets into the air to disperse the crowd.

That was when one of the corporals saw a boy who could have been a university student; he was carrying a knapsack. The area was deserted now, and the boy was walking briskly between the stones and the tear gas. The corporal thought he looked suspicious. His inspector had gone to ease himself in the nearby bush, so the corporal beckoned to him. "Hey-shhh, come here." The boy acted like he didn't see or hear the corporal. "Hey-shh, you there carrying bag, come here now!" The boy kept walking. The corporal rushed toward him in a fit of rage and whacked the boy from behind with the butt of his gun at the base of the neck, and the boy went down at once. "Bagger!" the corporal barked as the boy's body dropped to the ground.

"Wetin be that?" the other colleagues questioned him.

"I dey ask this bastard to come, him dey ignore me."

One of them went toward the boy lying on the ground and stooped over him. "Wetin you do am? E be like say you don wound the boy-o."

A constable joined them to lift the boy as they put him in their van. They tapped him on the cheeks, shouted things at him in order to revive him.

The inspector came back and asked what was going on. They said the boy looked suspicious and they had tried to stop him. He wouldn't stop, and a little accident occurred when the corporal went over to accost him. The inspector bent over the unconscious boy in the back of the van and was the first to notice the trickle of blood from his ears and nose. He turned around and spat abuses at the corporal. He threatened to ensure that the corporal got sacked if things turned for the worse. "You have injured an innocent boy! Let's hope nothing happens to him. What do you mean, he looked suspicious?"

By the time they decided to take the injured boy to the military hospital near Rumuola, he had stopped breathing.

At about two-thirty P.M., the superintendent placed a call to his elder brother, who was the chief superintendent in charge of the Port Harcourt area. He went about everything with a calmness that suggested he might have done this many times. They searched the boy's bag in hope of seeing anything that might incriminate him, but they only found cassette tapes, comic books, a Sony Walkman, and a video club card with a name and address on the back: Paul Utu, 11 Yakubu Gowon Avenue, Port Harcourt.

By evening, the affair was concluded, and they penned down a report: The boy had been caught looting a shop during the demonstration, an officer tried to stop him, and he assaulted the officer with a knife. A struggle ensued, during which the suspect went for the officer's gun. Unfortunately, there was an accidental discharge and a bullet struck the suspect, killing him instantly. The two-page report was filed away.

The body of the deceased was quickly designated to the fate of armed robbers: A hole was dug at the back of the mopol station, and the body was tossed inside. It got dark quickly that day, well before six o'clock.

⌛

Of everything Ma had fought through in her life—the challenges of her childhood, her education, her early marriage, the birth of her children, her husband's illness—there was no time she fought harder, more viciously, and with more focus than she did in the days after the ex–mopol pastor came to reveal what had happened to Paul.

She was on the phone early the next day, making arrangements. By eight A.M. two days later, she was waiting in the anteroom of the governor's office, having secured an appointment with the help of former colleagues and friends. By the Thursday before Ajie arrived, she had obtained permission to dig in search of Paul's body in the plot of land behind the fence of the police station. Colleagues and friends rallied around her, offering all kinds of assistance. Someone drove down to the family's former dentist in Bolokiri to get Paul's records. Someone else had a relative who worked at a new hospital in Abuja where a DNA test could be done to confirm whether the bones they had exhumed were Paul's remains.

CHAPTER TWENTY-FIVE

The taxi driver has no change, so Bibi runs inside while her boyfriend stands beside their bags. She shouts at Ajie to give her two hundred naira; she grabs the money from him and tosses a thousand-naira note at him. "Look at you, looking so proper!" she says to him with a twinkle in her eyes.

Ajie follows her outside. Bibi says, "This is my runaway brother you have heard so much about. Dotun, Ajie."

Ajie and Dotun nod at each other and shake hands. Dotun lifts the two suitcases and leaves Bibi with only her handbag; Ajie takes one of the suitcases from him, and they make their way into the house.

Dotun seems eager but relaxed. Ajie looks at his carefully brushed hair and the sharp creases at the back of his striped shirt and decides that Dotun might have had a strict upbringing. He must have been raised by the sort of parents who were excessive with discipline but generous, however, with any sort of expenditure relating to schooling, self-improvement, and getting ahead in life. He fabricates Dotun's family history even though he knows little about him. Bibi mentioned she met Dotun in the medical school library at the University of Ibadan, where they both studied. Seeing him, Ajie decides even that minor fact seems fitting. Dotun is the kind of boy who meets a girl at the library and then finds himself years later halfway across the country in order to meet her family.

Dotun steps into the parlor first and almost collides with Ma, who is coming out to meet them. She is startled and then beams at him, saying several welcomes, touching him by the shoulders, and asking how he is. The Utus have never been a family of huggers or kissers, but Ma falls into Bibi's arms once she sees her, and Bibi wraps her arms around her, too, and it looks as if they will remain so forever.

The next morning at the funeral home, the undertaker leaves them alone in the room and shuts the door. Ma picked the casket herself. It is nothing flashy, just dark polished wood. The inside is padded with red velvet, and there are silver handles on the sides and the lid.

They have waited many years for an answer, and one has finally arrived, dry and diminished, resting inside the wooden box before them, and not one of them in the room knows how to approach the coffin. Ajie feels it's his place to take the lead; he steps forward to the casket and opens it. When Ma draws close, he holds her hand while Bibi looks in from the other side of the casket. He holds Ma's hand tight but can still feel the tremor running through it. *These bones formed inside her,* Ajie thinks. Bibi is the one who has received training over the past seven years on how to handle a human body. She must have spent enough time seeing how the human body can go wrong, how it can turn against itself, how it heals, grows, rots, and what it looks like once the flesh has fallen away. It is Bibi who leans close and touches Paul. Ma has informed the undertakers that they would prefer to arrange what is left of the body themselves.

"Lock the gate," Ma goes outside to tell Ismaila after they get home. "If anyone comes, tell them we are not available. They can come back next week."

"Yes, madam," Ismaila says.

Ma joins everyone else in the parlor and sits down. Her face is still puffy and damp, her hands still tremble. Her eyes are welling up with tears again. Bibi's face is turned toward Dotun, who has pulled his chair back a little bit.

"Whatever Paul went out for that day," Ma continues, "it's fine. I have settled it with my God. I mean, he was a child, and maybe he just wanted to go out and see. What I'm saying is that I don't think he would want us to sit and mourn." Dotun is nodding gravely and looking at Ma as she speaks. Ajie looks at Bibi and can't read her at all—her eyes look tired but placid.

Ajie picks up a newspaper and goes to sit in the dining area. It is left to Dotun to initiate a conversation. He is mourning with this grieving family, but he also wants to take their minds off things.

"How is the work going?" he asks Ma. "Bibi said you have been working on a book about plants."

"What?" Ma asks, looking like she's been startled out of sleep.

"The book you are writing."

"Yes, yes. It's a scrapbook. I've been collecting some plant samples," she says. "They are all probably going to go extinct from the area in a few years." Her face comes alive. "I have a friend at the University of Port Harcourt who is typing it up and converting the pictures to electronic files."

Ajie props the newspaper before him. How should he read it? He flips past a story about a Briton who was kidnapped by gunmen who are now demanding a ransom. He skims through the business page and reads an interview of a man who began the first online shopping business in the country, and it is all talk of markets and huge potential and challenges.

"Do you have a title for it yet?" Dotun keeps on.

"I was hoping to get suggestions from these ones." Ma gestures toward her children. "The title I have is a little long: *Ferns and Fauna of the Orashi Plain.*"

"I like it," Bibi says.

"Ma, that's a very good title," Paul says, and Ajie turns around to look at him, but Paul is not there. Paul is dead, and what is left of him is in a casket at a funeral home near St. John's.

Apart from Dotun, who is sitting in the armchair, everything else in the parlor looks exactly the same as when they were children. Ma has returned the family photographs to the wall. She took them all down years ago, after Paul disappeared and Bendic passed away. Now she has replaced the family portrait. Her wedding photo is right below the wall clock. They are standing in front of the St. Luke's Cathedral in Ede. Ma is dressed in an ivory satin dress and Bendic is wearing a gray suit. A white flower is pinned to the lapel of his suit.

Paul, Bibi, and Ajie are in a photograph hanging in the dining area. Bibi has a small frown on her face. There was something phenomenal about her rage when she was about eight or nine years old. It whipped about for what seemed just over a moment until she snapped and double-slapped you in the face, but here she is now, a recently qualified doctor, collected, her cornrows neat and sheeny.

In the picture, Paul is smiling and ready for the camera. He is looking at Bendic, who is standing outside the frame, telling Ajie to adjust his collar. Ajie looks away from the photo and back at the newspaper before him. He suddenly realizes he is gasping for breath and silently whooping. He puts his head down, and his tears free-fall into the pages and smudge the black print. He stands up, walks into the kitchen, and turns the tap on.

When he returns to the living room, he says, "I think I will go to Ogibah tomorrow, Ma. So I get there a day before you all to get things ready. You haven't been to the house for a while now. Besides, I want to check out what they've done about the grave."

"I wanted you to be in the car that's taking your brother."

"I know, but someone needs to be there to make sure everything is in place."

"It's true," Ma says. Then she warns Ajie to be careful in Ogibah. "Things aren't the way they used to be." Disputes are no longer settled with raised voices in a meeting. People no longer write strongly worded petitions to voice their dissent. If you disagree with someone these days, you simply go over to the person's house with your face unmasked and shoot him. OYF has split into warring factions, and the body count is on a steep rise.

The bike speeds past the church and comes to a halt as it reaches the house. Ajie gets off and hands the *okada* man some cash and waits for his change.

"The people wey get here no dey come home again," the man says to him as he rifles through his pockets for change.

Ajie wants to say something in Ogba so the bike man stops taking him for a stranger. He wants to tell the man to mind his own business, but he doesn't. He just smiles and waits for his change. He imagines the man's reaction if he speaks in Ogba. First surprise that he speaks the language at all, and then that he speaks it well. He would want to know who Ajie is, and Ajie is in no mood to be fawned over. He collects his change from the bike man and turns to leave.

"I am Ofuma by name." The man is relentless. Ajie accepts the challenge but plays it his own way—he won't be forced to introduce himself. The paint of the house is peeling and the roofing sheets are rotten and exposed in parts. It is midday, and a kit of pigeons squawk and fly out of a gap on the roof.

"Oga Ofuma, safe journey," Ajie says to the bike man and walks toward the house, his bag heavy and swaying from his shoulders. He walks beneath the eaves of the house and then looks back at the motorcycle as it makes its way past the church, past the fruit tree by the road, lost in the distance.

Bendic's grave is to the right side of the quadrangle, and beside it, on the left, is the one made for Paul.

Once Ajie has put his things away, he goes over to Nne Nta's house to greet her and stays only long enough to tell her everyone is well and that Ma and the others will arrive the next morning, before giving an excuse to leave to attend to an urgent matter.

Ossai's mother is not at home when Ajie gets there. He meets a little boy who tells him she has gone to the farm and that Ossai is attending a polytechnic in Warri. Company, the boy tells him, awarded twenty scholarships to Ogibah people, and Ossai was one of the lucky ones to get picked.

Ajie doesn't meet anyone on the road as he makes his way back home. Most people are on their farms by this time of day. The walk seems shorter than he remembers it.

He leaves the house behind, ambles toward the churchyard. He greets the warden at the church, and the man hesitates to ask him who he is. Ajie continues on his way. "Don't be offended," the man calls behind him. "Are you not Benedict's son?"

"I am," Ajie replies, "the second one."

"God Almighty!" The man cups his hand over his mouth. "Carbon copy! Exactly like your father."

He asks Ajie about the burial, and Ajie tells him it's tomorrow. His mother wants it as quiet as possible. A small service and interment. They've prepared only light refreshments for the guests, unlike normal funerals.

"We will be there," the man says firmly. "Me and my family. I don't think you will remember me. You were so small when you people came home last."

"Of course I remember you." Ajie smiles and says the man's name.

"That is good!" The man beams. "Wonderful. So where are you going now? You can come to my house when you are free."

"I will," Ajie says. "I am just going to the swamp. The weather is too hot. I would like to get in the water."

"The swamp behind the school?"

"Yes," Ajie replies.

"It's gone. All the ponds are dried up," the man says. "You know they have built a dam across the river at Idu?"

"Who?"

"Nearly ten years now," with a slight shrug of the shoulder, like it was an event from long ago and he has forgotten how to feel about it.

"Who built the dam?" Ajie asks in a surprising surge of rage.

"My son, it wasn't even today Company built that dam; they offered to pay for the land, and the families who owned the land fought and fought among each other, but finally, the dam is there now."

But you can't buy up a stream, Ajie wants to say before he leaves the man to go on his way. You can't just buy up a stream or a swamp, a river, or any communal water body. Nobody has a right to do that. It surprises him—this spark of rage in his chest. Right now he would like to snap away something from someone, something dear to him or her, and destroy it completely. He would like to strike down whoever has made this happen, make them totally powerless to protect the thing they love, humiliate them, reduce them to trivial and useless things. What if he walks across the road now and stops any of these trucks passing with Company workers in them; if he is in luck, there might be someone in it senior enough to have been part of the decision to dam the river. He would order them out of the van and make like he has a gun in his pocket. Oh, the rush of actually having a gun to hold to a person's head. He would make them lie on the ground and step on their heads with his shoes to make sure their faces were rubbing in the dirt, and they would shiver with fear and maybe piss their pants, begging. How do you make someone feel useless and powerless, how do you make someone feel like a stupid worthless thing that has never mattered and never will? With this he marches across the road, beyond the school, which has been moved to a new site.

The swamp is not there. The ponds are dried up, all the trees felled. No slowworms, no bamboo or bracken, no blackbirds pecking on a rotting palm trunk. He walks on in what is now a rough stretch of land that he can see from here to there, and farther away new buildings being erected.

He walks through the length of it. When he returns home, the sun is cooling and he can hear people talking to each other as more people return from the farm. He decides against a shower, opting for bed instead. There is a stone in his heart, and the weight of it sinks deep and makes his legs weary.

Few people have a treasure. He must have read this somewhere, and he will tell it to anyone he loves, or his children, for that matter, if he gets to have any. *Few people, very few, have a treasure, and if they do, they must cling to it and not let themselves be ambushed and have it taken from them.*

Even though he feels this strongly, he is no longer certain whether the words are true or useful. And where is Paul when Ajie is in need of certainty?

CHAPTER TWENTY-SIX

He wakes up twice at night and falls back into a recurring dream.

He is nine years old again and Paul is sitting beside him on the mud floor in Nkaa's front room. It is the night of *ntitroegberi,* and Nkaa is to narrate—as he does once every year—the story of how their ancestors came to Ali-Ogba. On such nights, the room is usually packed with people, but today's flow is scanty, some children half asleep, cross-legged on a mat. Kitchen stools with uneven legs are stacked on each other by the corner. There is a chill in the air, but the space is firelit; it crackles and leaps, shadows grow long on the mud walls.

Nkaa sweeps into the room in full regalia. Black velvet *feni* with yellow furry imprints of lion heads spewing fire. The wrapper tied around his waist is grazing the floor, stiff with embroidery, strewn with sequins and stones, and his red cap is adorned with a singular eagle feather. He approaches the armchair that has been set for him by the fire; he is magnificent and terrible, a towering old tree. He assumes his throne and makes a gesture designed to prompt silence, but this is not necessary.

Paul is sitting on Ajie's left side, and to Ajie's right is a boy who is reeking of palm kernel oil. Ajie hates the smell of palm kernel oil. The light from the flames makes the lion heads on Nkaa's tunic look bloodred.

Nkaa begins: Hundreds of years ago, in the royal courts of

the ancient Bini kingdom, Prince Ogualor is raging against his brothers, and there is no way to pacify him—the cause of his anger various and unclear. He goes in search of them in the palaces. Nkaa suffers genuine alarm, his hand flies up and slams against his chest as he recounts the tale, for Ogualor's temper was legendary. It is a night of anger and blood, of treachery, betrayal, and separation. He growls like a wounded leopard, picks up his machete, and goes in hunt of his brothers. Prince Ogualor ransacks the land; he splits in half any man he meets on his way. Wherever he goes, a wilderness follows in his wake. His brother Aklaka hears of the hunt and flees Bini. He takes his sons, Ogba and Ekpeye. In order not to be discovered, they travel in disguise and without their retinue down the River Niger. They fake their lives as ordinary people, mere travelers, a people displaced by famine or war. They search for a place beyond the reach of Prince Ogualor; for a spell, they settle among people they meet on the way. They lie down for a season in Agbor, but news reaches them that Ogualor has not relented in his search, so they pack up and move down the Niger River.

Decades go by, and Aklaka grows gray and frail. Before he passes away, the gods show him a vision of the land his children will settle on. It is the center of the earth. Igmi is to the right, Oru to the left. It is between the great forests and the endless sea. The land is fertile and the water rich with fish.

They travel on till they dip their feet in the Sombreiro. The river is quick and aloof. They pass through the land of the Engenni. They marry wives from their neighbors. Is Aboh not their brother? What about all those who reside near the water? Is Awura not to them as a sister? Is Oguta not just here beside us? They set down on the plains between the great rivers Orashi and Sombreiro, gently sloping and well drained. They make their first home in Ahiahu.

Nkaa breaks into singing; his voice is smoky, and he taps his fingers on his wrapper, inspiring a response from his audience.

Paul nudges Ajie awake. He elbows him gently three times, and the bedspring creaks as Ajie rolls over on his side. The morning sun catches his eyes.

Everything is going well. The sound system has been set up successfully, four canopies pitched around in the quadrangle, and people are seated already, waiting for the pastor to begin the funeral service with a prayer. Ma is sitting on a bench beside the casket, her hand resting on the lid's silver handle, as if she needs to steady it from falling off.

There is a crowd, but Ajie doesn't notice anyone in particular. Deaths always draw a crowd, funerals draw larger crowds, and funerals for people who passed away in dramatic circumstances draw the largest crowds.

People push their way toward him. They talk, offer condolences, touch him on his shoulders—strangers, family, friends, all in beautiful dark clothes. His eyes cut through the array of them, their essence yielded up to him, but he doesn't drink them in. He feels like he is all eyes. He has never seen as clearly as he does today. His old friend Gospel is testing the microphone, and Bibi hurries past with a tray of refreshments. That's just Bibi being her capable self, making sure everyone is catered to. A lump rises in Ajie's throat; his rib cage is about to heave. Dotun walks over to ask if he and Gospel need any help, and Ajie says no, he has this one, but Dotun still stands by as Ajie switches the mic on and off and taps it and adjusts a button on the feedback speaker.

A girl Ajie does not care to remember is wailing by the pavement; she is sitting on the floor with her legs stretched out, bawling. Her cry becomes a song, and people gather around to console her. Older people in Ogibah, it seems, still stay away from the funeral of a very young person. Dying young is always considered an indecent act that should be met with proportionate rudeness so it doesn't repeat itself. Application Master came to see Ma that morning and stayed with her for a while. He has gone home, saying he would return later. The girl weeping by the pavement has broken into a mourning dance, swaying and waving an invisible handkerchief this way and that way like someone paddling a canoe. This inspires sobs from other mourners, all of them showing up at a funeral and weeping louder than the bereaved. Bibi walks by the mourners, and one of them holds her by the waist, and Bibi pauses and touches her slightly on the back. Were they childhood friends? Ajie decides he does not know any of them. If he tells Bibi what he is thinking, she will say he has spent too much time abroad and has grown impatient with Ogibah ways.

He is very thirsty. Like he hasn't had a drop to drink in the past thirteen years. All he needs right now is a cold bottle of Guinness or half a glass of stinging whiskey. He is desperate for a cigarette, but he knows there is no quenching that. The dead will not be consoled; neither will those who live in the skin of their dead.

Some people have traveled from very far; many have come on the shortest notice, as soon as they heard. They tell Ajie all these things and look him in the face and hold his hand. Ma couldn't reach Mr. Ifenwa, since he moved back to his home village, Nnobi.

The pastor is standing by the lectern now and, after a short prayer, reads a verse from Job 19 and a couple of verses from I Corinthians 15. They all rise to sing from a hymnbook. Ma picked the hymn herself. She deliberated over three final choices and then selected a favorite from her school days, "Be Still My Soul." Ajie mouths the words of the hymn as the assembly sings along. He looks at Ma, standing beside the casket, the funeral program fluttering a little in her hand.

> *Be still, my soul; the Lord is on thy side;*
> *Bear patiently the cross of grief or pain;*
> *Be still, my soul; thy God doth undertake*
> *To guide the future as He has the past . . .*

The casket is lowered into the ground just as the church bells strike one.

Back in Port Harcourt later that evening, Ajie reaches for the school bag in the wardrobe. He wonders how it is possible to have Paul's school bag returned to them after such a long time. In a place where things vanish without explanation, where all the wrong things are always waiting to happen, the miracle of having Paul's bag in his hand now makes him wonder. He holds himself back from examining or handling the contents. He puts the bag in the wardrobe.

Bibi is sitting on the veranda with Dotun. They are talking about Braithwaite Memorial Hospital, where Bibi will be starting her residency program. They are both moving down from Ibadan, where they studied, to Port Harcourt. Ma is in the back garden, reading aloud to herself from the lesson for next Sunday school. As Ajie steps into the parlor, he picks up some of the words Ma is reading. He tries to follow her sentences, but they dance on the limits of his mind.

Ma's typed manuscripts are stacked on the dining table. *Ferns and Faunas of the Orashi Plain.* He thinks of the specimens in the book: Even if they become extinct, at least a memory of them has been preserved and can be called to life any day. He wonders if there is a bigger volume somewhere, a roll of every living thing, past and present, gathered, standing in their cohort: fungi, plants, animals, in families, genera, species, and variants. He is still thinking about this when Ma's voice comes again from the back of the house. "Bibi," she calls out. Ma is looking toward the house. She has taken off her reading glasses. "It's evening already, Bibi. Please put something on the fire. We have to eat."

Ajie reaches for the light switch on the parlor wall and turns it on.

ACKNOWLEDGMENTS

Sodienye Kurubo, my friend and my most exacting critic, who read this book first, in draft, and many times over; for his sharp eyes and good heart, for the angry-red notes that helped this book become what it is. Thank you, Sodi. How I for do?

For their love and support, for honoring my need for space, for never sharing their worry about me squandering time, I thank my family: *Osa umu ka Edi-nwa-Ile,* especially Dadu Fearn; I salute all the Iles of Obagi (*Nde guzo a guzo!*); Georgia and Joshua Fearn, for making me laugh.

I owe an enormous debt of gratitude to many friends who read drafts, gave keys to their flats, forgave when I didn't return calls or respond to e-mails and text messages, bought my round of drinks while I looked away: Adiela Orike (dear cousin-brother, for giving me my first home away from home), Jonah Dienye, Bobby Obi, Sylvia Ofili, Nnachi Nnachi, Yemi Akinwale (that Yoruba boy), Owukori Akuyibo, Mfoniso Udosen, Teinane Okpokiti, Abiodun Okunola, Bassey Essien, Philip Iyayi, Niyi Famuboni, Naakuu Paul-Birabi (self-declared "Afropolitan with Anglo-Saxon work ethic"—ha!), Gérard Tetegan, Boma Koko, Biebele Okpokiri, and Ilami Onyekwum, wherever she may be.

I thank Chimamanda Adichie for her matchless generosity of spirit; Ike Anya, waterer of seed; John Bond, for the kindness of that e-mail; Dominic Reilly, for speaking with me in Dothraki, and for much more.

Thank you to my agent, Sarah Chalfant, who makes the world seem easier than it really is; to Alba Ziegler-Bailey and Jacqueline Ko. I am grateful to Tim Duggan, my judicious editor; to Thomas Gebremedhin and everyone at Tim Duggan Books.